Hearts on Fire

Dogs, Love, and Calendar Heroes

(Recipes for Love and Life)

A Novella

Joanna Slodownik

Table of Contents

1.

A loud ring tone wakes me up from shallow dreaming. I pick up the phone without opening my eyes.

"Olivia! You must come right now!" My best friend's voice sounds alarmed.

"Penelope? What's up?" I yawn and stretch my legs. I must have dozed off on my couch in front of the television. I glance at my watch. It's half-past midnight.

"The shelter is on fire!"

I jolt up and sit up straight, suddenly wide awake. "Did you call the fire department?"

"They're here. Plus, the police and two ambulances, and a bunch of reporters."

"I'm coming!" I'm still in my day clothes, so I don't even have to change. While searching for my shoes, I reach for the remote and switch to the local news. "Oh, no," I groan. The place looks in total disarray. I see flames and firefighters carrying dogs and cats out from the kennels. It's a total disaster! "Ruffy!" I exclaim as I see a close-up of one of my beloved dogs appear on the screen.

"Ruffy is fine," Penelope says. "One of the firefighters saved him."

"I know! I'm watching the local news. How bad is it?"

"Most animals seem okay. The fire department got here super fast. But we must move the animals away from the smoke. Hold on," she says, and I hear loud voices in the background.

"What's going on there?"

"I'll talk to you later," she says and disconnects.

I grab my car keys and rush out the door. I can't believe that the place so dear to my heart is in danger. Those animals have been through so much, suffering pain and misery their entire lives. And now this! I'm not religious, but I start praying to God to save them.

There's no traffic at this hour, so I arrive at the shelter in record time, slowing down only at the intersections to avoid getting stopped by the police. Although with the fire in the neighborhood, I'd be shocked if cops stopped me for speeding. I imagine they have more important things to do than to chase reckless drivers.

When I arrive at the Kind Heart Animal Shelter, two fire trucks are there, plus three police cars and an ambulance.

The barking and howling of the animals are unbearable. The smoke fills the air, and the fire trucks' lights make the scene surreal, but the situation appears under control.

"Olivia! Over here!" Penelope calls me from a distance. "Thank the heavens that the station is so close; they got here in no time," she says when I approach her. She points to the group of firefighters who are now packing their gear, getting ready to leave.

Then she points in another direction. "That's Ryan Kowalski. He saved Ruffy and the other dogs from section C-1, which suffered the most damage. He's not unpleasant to look at either."

I shoot her an appalled look. How can she be thinking about those things when the situation is so dramatic?

"Aren't you still seeing Mark?" I ask.

"I'm just saying. Maybe you'll be interested."

"Thanks, but no," I reply with a tone of annoyance in my voice. She knows I'm not interested in men, but she keeps trying to set me up for my own good, as she says. "How are the animals?" I ask.

"It looks like the firefighters did a great job. Thanks to them, there was no major damage to the kennels. We should thank them."

I shrug. "Isn't that their job?"

Barbara Johnson, the shelter director, comes up to us, shaking her head in distress. "How could this happen? A fire can't just start by itself. Did someone leave on the toaster? I told you we should have got rid of that thing; it's defective."

"I switched off all the appliances in the lunchroom before I left, so that wasn't it," says Penelope.

"Do the police know what caused the fire?" I ask.

Penelope shakes her head. "They suspect it started somewhere behind the back office building, but they don't know for sure. The dog's kennels closest to the fire got burned, but we took all the animals out just in time. A few of our volunteers are here helping the animals. Some of the dogs got really scared."

"Who notified the fire department?" Barbara asks.

"I did," says Penelope. "I went back to the office to take the applications of adoption to review tonight. That's when I saw the smoke and called 911."

Barbara sighs heavily and shakes her head. "This is a disaster."

We all nod in agreement.

"As if we didn't have enough problems already."

2.

After the night in the shelter, I go home totally exhausted, home being Eric's two-bedroom apartment. After I broke up with my boyfriend six months ago, I didn't have a place to go. Thankfully, my friend Eric let me stay with him until I find a new place, which was taking longer than I expected. People may tell you that they love animals, but no one seems to want a tenant with three dogs, two cats, and a bunny.

I really love him for that. Eric is a great guy, and I don't say it often about men, if ever. He's also different than most men. For one, he's gay, so our relationship is purely platonic.

As I collapse on my bed, my three adopted dogs come into the room and start licking my hands, nudging me with their cold, wet noses. I try to hide under the blanket. I only have a few hours to sleep before I go back to the shelter again.

But they don't go away. I can hear their expectant panting. As I peek from under the cover, Charlie, Oscar, and Coco wave their tails at me.

"Alright, you win. You must be hungry, huh?" I get up with resignation and go to the kitchen to fill their bowls. Then I find the remote and turn on the television. The fire is all over the local channels.

"Officials are trying to determine the cause of the fire that happened last night at the Kind Heart Animal shelter on Harrison Road. Firefighters with the Essex County Fire and Rescue told us that one of the buildings had flames shooting through the roof when they arrived at the scene. Firefighters were joined by the shelter workers, volunteers, and private citizens, trying to rescue as many animals from the structure as possible. Fire officials tell us they do not have an immediate need to care for the animals, but they may need help soon. The shelter director,

Barbara Johnson, noted that a few shelters stepped up, offering help taking animals into their care, including the Essex Animal shelter."

"Look, it's Barbara on the news," I shout out to Eric, who is in the shower. The reporter puts the mike in front of Barbara, who says, "We are very grateful for their generous offer, but we believe we'll be able to keep all our animals in our shelter, which they regard as their home. Moving them elsewhere would only cause them additional distress. Thanks to the quick reaction of the fire department, most animals are okay, and the kennels didn't suffer any major damage. We'll be setting up some tents as temporary adoption office facilities and resume the normal operations shortly."

All the while, they're showing the video footage from last night. The imagery is dramatic. The fire, the animals, the firefighters.

Especially one firefighter.

What's his name? Ryan something. He's rescuing Ruffy over and over and over again, carrying him in his arms with fire gushing behind him, like an action hero in a Hollywood movie. Then there is a close-up, with Ryan's face and a big smile.

"Enough already," I groan and flip the channel.

But there it is again, a close-up of Ryan Kowalski's smiling face. It isn't even a proper smile, more like a smirk.

"He's very photogenic," Eric says.

"And he knows it."

I try another channel. And another. It's the same thing everywhere, as if he were the only one there that night.

"Ryan Kowalski is obviously getting his five minutes of fame," I say as I flip through the channels. The same clips are playing on all the local news channels. Reporters (mostly female) are going on and on about how the firefighters saved the animals, gushing about how fortunate the poor dogs were to be rescued by such heroic humans.

"Oh, please," I groan. I can't help but roll my eyes at all that adoration. "This is so annoying. Can you just tell me some real news? Like who or what started the fire?" I say to the reporter on the screen.

"Oh, come on," says Eric. "They deserve it. Don't you think what they did was admirable?"

"Sure. I'm deeply thankful to them. But, seriously. Enough already! It's their job for crying out loud. Plus, the fire wasn't even that bad, and they're making it into some sort of a super-freaking-hero on a mission-impossible situation. Isn't all that admiration a bit too much?"

Eric nods. "Maybe. They seem to enjoy it, though."

We watch as Ryan Kowalski and his crew are posing for pictures with dogs and cats from the shelter, talking to reporters who treat them as if they're gods. "See? This bothers me," I say.

"What about it?" asks Eric.

I shrug. "It bothers me is that it's just another piece of news that people will forget as soon as another disaster comes around."

"That's the way things are…"

"I know. But the truth is no one cares about the life and death of these animals. Not before and not now. Many of them are going to be killed, maybe even next week or month, because there's just not enough space and no money to keep them alive in the shelter. And not enough people are willing to adopt or donate money."

"Euthanasia is the politically correct term," Eric says.

"Which is really the same thing," I say. "Every day, hundreds of dogs and cats are euthanized in the United States, but no freaking reporters are bringing the story to the public. There's no video coverage about those killings on the news. Volunteers, rescue workers, shelter employees, and other individuals work their butts off every day to find adoptive homes for these animals, struggling to save their lives, but no one congratulates them or treats them as heroes."

"Well…" Eric starts, but I'm not done with my rant.

"Okay, so we don't have to risk their own lives and don't wear cute uniforms, but we make sacrifices too, giving up our time and money to help those animals, often at the expense of our personal lives and careers. No reporter or journalist came to the shelter to write about that, ever."

"Someone is feeling unappreciated," Eric says.

"It's not just about that," I protest.

"Then what?"

"Everyone is so freaking excited about the fact that the firemen saved the animals; only what's going to happen to them now? If nobody wants them, they're going to end up dead anyway." I shake my head in frustration. "They've been saved from a fire only to die—from an injection. And it seems like everyone is okay with that. Is dying in fire different than being killed by euthanasia?" I ask.

"Less painful probably, but other than that? Death is death."

"Why don't people come and save them themselves? It's easy," I say. "Adopt. Foster. Volunteer. They could be heroes, too."

"That's not newsworthy. Not dramatic enough."

"Okay, I get it. There's no fire gushing in the background. Nothing heroic about it. Just mouths to feed. And poops to scoop."

Eric chuckles. "No one will show you on the prime-time TV doing that!"

3.

"You need to get a life beyond the shelter, Olivia. The whole world doesn't revolve just about cats, dogs, pigs, and rabbits," Eric says.

"Tell me something I don't know," I mutter.

Life has to go on after the fire, and things are getting back to normal, which means we're washing off dog poop and pee off the kennel's floors with a stream of cold water from a hose.

"Life is short. Forgive me for stating the obvious, but there you go."

"Wow, aren't you a sage today?" I say sarcastically. "What's come over you?"

"Life is short," Eric repeats. "It creeps up on you like a thief in the night. Things happen you never expected. But every once and a while, the skies open up, and you can see that clear path ahead of you."

I look at him suspiciously. "Are you okay?"

He nods. "You need a relationship with a human. Not a cat, not a dog. A man," he says.

"Look who is talking," I grouch. "You want me to move out, and I will, I promise. Eventually." My dogs and I have overstayed our welcome, which is why I've been looking for a new job that will help me pay for a place that accepts pets while leaving me enough time to volunteer at the shelter.

Eric shakes his head. "It's not about that. I'm just saying life is short. Way too damn short to spend it alone."

"Are we still talking about me?" I ask. I know that Eric has broken up with his partner of three years because he found him cheating with a woman. It was over a year ago, and he still can't get over it. "Because if we are, then you need to know that I already have a man in my life—" I say, giving Eric a fake grin and pointing the hose at him. "You!"

"Hey! Stop!" he screams, jumping up and down to avoid the stream of ice-cold water. I turn the hose back into the next kennel to wash more poops.

Eric fake-grins back at me. "You know what I mean. A relationship with a straight man, who will sweep you off your feet and carry you into the scorching-red sunset."

"Scorching red sunset? Oh, please, Eric. Where do you get your metaphors?" I sneer. "You know, I've had enough relationships with men, thank you. They didn't work. And—sorry to say that—they didn't work for you either."

Eric shrugs. "Maybe you're right, but it doesn't mean that I'm ready to throw in the towel," he says. "Never give up, never surrender is my philosophy. Can you pass me that towel?" He motions to the towel hanging on the bench.

I pick it up and give it to him. "That whole dating-love-marriage thing isn't for me. I don't want to waste any more time. I prefer to spend it doing something useful and meaningful with my life…"

"Like washing off poop?"

"It's an important job, and somebody has to do it," I say and stomp my foot in the puddle, splashing the water all over my pants, and we both laugh. "And—I happen to be an excellent poop washer," I point out, raising my chin high proudly. "Besides, men are liars and cheaters. There may be exceptions, of course, such as you, but those are rare. Animals, on the other hand…"

"I know, I know. Animals won't cheat or lie to you or laugh at you behind your back, as people do," Eric says, mocking me. "You should stop being so negative. The fact that your relationship with Christian didn't work out is not proof that it won't work with somebody else. It's not healthy to be bitter and isolate yourself from the whole world," Eric says.

"If you walked in on your boyfriend cheating on you with a personal trainer, you'd be bitter too," I say.

Eric falls silent. "I'd probably be mad as hell," he finally says. "But you should look at the bright side; at least they weren't having sex."

"I'm sorry about what happened to you. But what Christian and that Anastasia girl were doing was way worse," I snap.

"Okay, so Christian hurt your feelings, but you need to get over it. You must go out and meet more people and loosen up a little. Remember, nobody is perfect. Nobody can live up to your high standards. And even if you make a mistake along the way, that's okay, too. At least you're giving yourself a chance to find Mr. Right eventually."

I shrug and open another kennel to wash. What could Eric possibly know about relationships with straight men? Not much.

We finish washing the floors in silence. After we're done, Eric makes sure all the doors are locked while I put away the hoses. We then walk back to what is left of the office of the Kind Heart animal shelter.

Even though I'm just a volunteer, it feels like the shelter is my second home. Maybe even my first, since I give all my heart to these animals, spending there as much time as I can, to the point some say I practically live there and currently have no apartment or house of my own.

Hmm. If I'm between apartments, does that make me a homeless person? I don't have any income to speak of either since I'm in-between jobs. Working at the shelter is practically the only thing I do, except eating, sleeping, living off my savings ever since I decided to quit my job at the law office to look for a less soul-drenching career. (If I had to defend another cheating husband or dishonest businessman, I would just have to commit seppuku, which means I'll kill myself unless I'd go mad first and would have to be committed to a psychiatric institution.)

Penelope is sitting in front of her laptop in the office. She works at one of the top advertising agencies in town and volunteers at the shelter, coming there three times per week to walk the dogs because she loves animals so much. She only has a cat and can't have a dog because the building association makes the lives of pet owners difficult. (I hate the term pet owner. But is there a better one? The caretaker, perhaps. But that sounds dry.)

"I'm making coffee," she announces, pouring tap water into the pot. "Does anyone want some?"

"I do." Eric raises his hand.

"Olivia? How about you?" Penelope asks.

"No, thanks," I reply. I turn on the television to see any news about the police investigation into the fire. At least that's a distraction from the topic of my pitiful love life.

They don't have any new facts and are still replaying the clip of the fireman who rescued Ruffy, praising the firemen as the main heroes. The footage looks dramatic. Almost like it was photoshopped or whatever software they use to edit video. It certainly doesn't look like the actual event that I saw.

From what I remembered, it was much less spectacular, mostly a whole lot of smoke. But the presenters are going on and on about how courageous the firefighters are. If it weren't for them, the poor creatures would have been dead for sure.

I roll my eyes and turn the television sound to mute. I take out a pile of forms to fill out before Barbara gets there. As the aroma of brewing coffee starts to fill the room, I wonder whether I should have some after all. I've been trying to kick the caffeine addiction and drink freshly made juices and smoothies in the morning instead, but this is not the time or place to start new habits.

I take out my mug, place it on the table next to Eric's cup, and wait for the coffee to finish brewing. Caffeine to boost my energy after a sleepless night is just what I need.

4.

"Wow, look at him! Doesn't he look amazing?" Eric gasps, combing his perfectly manicured fingers through his hair. His fingernails look much better than mine, I notice. I know Eric frequents the "Tipsy Tips" manicure place that's next to the shelter, which I never do. Manicure is such a waste of time and money, in my opinion. Just as a hairstylist. I only go to cut my hair when I absolutely have to.

"Yeah, totally," Penelope says. "He's hot! What do you think, Olivia?"

I glance at the television screen, where the pictures of Ryan carrying Ruffy are still in full display. Then the camera closes up on Ruffy, as the presenter keeps recounting the events of last night.

"Of course, he is, totally," I say. Ruffy is an adorable creature, but I'm surprised by my friends' reaction. Penelope isn't that crazy about dogs; she's more of a cat person.

"And look at those muscles!" Eric says. "I wonder if he's straight."

Muscles? Straight? "Are we talking about Ruffy?" I ask disoriented.

Everybody bursts out laughing.

"Hell, no!" Penelope snorts. "We're talking about Ryan Kowalski. He's steaming hot."

"Smoking hot, if you know what I mean," Eric winks at her emphatically.

"And he's a hero," Penelope adds.

I roll my eyes at these two. "So he rescued a dog. Now everybody is gushing about what he did like it's such a huge deal," I say, annoyed. "Too bad the shelter wasn't on the news when we had to euthanize all these animals last month because nobody wanted them."

They fall silent because what is there to say? They know it's true. The shelter's walls aren't made of rubber; they can't stretch to accommodate all the animals that people breed and then throw away, like last year's Christmas presents.

"They talk about the fire like it was some big thing. People don't care about millions of dogs that have to be killed in shelters because nobody wants to take them home. Where were all those heroes then? All those compassionate humans, good Samaritans? Why don't they come to our shelter and adopt? And don't even get me started about farm animals…" I pause my tirade and shake my head in frustration.

"Well, aren't you cheerful this morning," Penelope says, pouring coffee into mugs. I notice cute dog pictures on them with the local pet store logo and wonder how they got here.

"You know it's the truth. Of course, adopting a dog isn't going to win you the admiration of the masses. Saving a dog or a cat from death by euthanasia is not glamorous. Washing poop and pee off the kennel floors is not exciting. Feeding them, loving them, and cleaning up their messes—there's nothing newsworthy about it. You don't have to risk your life, that's for sure."

"Wow, he's even cuter in person, don't you think?" Eric says, looking out the window.

"Who?" I ask.

"Ryan Kowalski."

"How am I supposed to know?" I shrug.

"He's smoking hot," Eric says. "I wonder if he's straight."

"Totally!" Penelope says. "He looked so manly with Ruffy."

"How could you tell with all the protective gear he had on?" I ask.

"Oh, I can tell. He's definitely much better looking than that Christian of yours," Penelope gives me a nudge on the ribs. "If I weren't getting serious with Peter, I'd totally ask him out. Olivia, you should talk to him."

"I don't ever intend to meet him."

"Well, he is coming right here," Eric replies, pointing at the window.

I glance outside. A tall man is walking in the direction of the office. Ryan Kowalski. He's a bit rough around the edges but kind of attractive; if someone is into that tall, muscular, look-at-me, oh-I'm-so-cute-and-fully-aware-of-it type of guy.

Which I'm not. At least, not anymore.

But, damn. He does look good in person. Suddenly I feel panicky and get up quickly. "I have to go to check how the cats are doing. I promised Barbara I'd make sure they're okay."

Barbara looks at me, surprised as if she's trying to remember when she asked me that. I try to walk unhurriedly. I'm not running away, after all. I'm simply not interested in meeting the hero who rescued Ruffy. The reason being that I'm totally over men. And I don't intend to meet this one, no matter how many dogs he saved.

"You talk to him and see what he wants," I say to no one in particular, reaching for the doorknob.

Before I have the time to step outside, the door to the office flings open, and there he is. The hero. Ryan Kowalski, standing right before me, in his firefighter's glory.

He waits for a few seconds, being a gentleman, but as I just stand there like a clay statue, he decides to enter at the same moment as I try to leave. We both try to fit in through the narrow doorway and end up getting stuck, standing so close I can feel the heat of his body and the scent of his cologne. Whoa! That's much too close for my liking.

"Excuse me," I mumble and glance up at him. My eyes meet his for a split second, sending a bolt of electricity down my spine.

Now, what was that about? Is that my inner goddess trying to tell me something? I think with sarcasm.

Ever since I read the Fifty Shades of Grey, which Penelope practically forced me to do, I've been hearing those weird voices inside my head. I finally push through and step outside, and as I turn around to wave goodbye, I almost fall over a pile of burned wood lying on the path. Ryan Kowalski, the hero that he is, steps in fast enough. He catches me, and a broad smile appears on his face. "I got you," he says.

"Sorry," I mumble as I free myself from his arms and quickly walk toward the cat kennel entrance.

5.

The man who rescued Ruffy is good looking; I have to admit that, but so what? Handsome or not, I have to see how the cats are doing after the spay and neuter procedure a couple of days ago. I'm not going to be swept away by some firefighter's charms so easily.

Christian was good looking, too, with the muscular body of the personal trainer at the local Fit & Strong gym, but in the end, it didn't mean a thing.

Even though it has been several months since we broke up, I can still feel the rage and humiliation over what had happened.

It was such a cliché!

I came home early one day and found him with a Zumba instructor from a nearby gym in our bedroom. The very memory of them there, wrapped in my favorite sheets, made me want to scream. I had put them on just the night before for what I thought would be a romantic night. The night turned into an argument, and I asked Christian to sleep on the sofa in the spare bedroom, but it was still not reason enough to do what he did. Talk about betrayal!

I knew something was wrong even before I entered the apartment. Charlie, Oscar, and Coco were outside in the backyard (I asked Christian many times not to let them out when I wasn't there). Charlie and Oscar came from abusive homes and still had issues, and I didn't want neighbors complaining about the barking. I saw Christian's car parked in the street, which meant that he was home, even though he told me he would be at the gym with clients all day.

Something told me to be very quiet as I entered. Was it a premonition? I prefer to think about it as intuition. I wasn't spying on him, of course, and I didn't have a reason to believe that he was doing anything wrong. I was just checking if everything was okay.

I heard muffled voices coming from the bedroom. That's odd, I thought. Why would Christian take a visitor to our bedroom? Unless … I didn't finish my thought. I tiptoed through the living room, trying not to make a sound on the hardwood floors. I stopped by the door to the bedroom, which was slightly ajar, but not wide enough for me to see what was going on inside.

I tried to listen to the conversation to see if I could recognize who was inside. I heard Christian's voice. He was with a woman. Something about her voice sounded familiar.

I knew her!

It was that girl from the gym—the Zumba instructor who worked in the same gym as Christian. The two were so preoccupied with each other; they didn't even notice that someone entered the apartment, giving me ample time to come up with a plan.

Christian and I had been together for six months, which was long considering my dating record. We met at the gym, and after just a couple of weeks, we decided to move in together when my landlord kicked me out because of my dogs. Now I wondered how many other personal training sessions like this he held in our bedroom.

"All she cares about are her dogs. She doesn't even care about me," I heard Christian's voice. He sounded so … whiny. "Umm, yes! This is perfect!" he grunted and then continued. "Her dogs are so messed up. They always bark at me. I'm afraid to go even to go to the bathroom at night."

"That's the problem if you take dogs from the shelter. You don't know where they came from. It's so much better to buy from a breeder or a pet store. At least you know what you're getting."

A moment of silence followed. What were they doing in there? I hesitated whether I should come in and let them know I was there.

"She works all the time and never has any fun. She works at her day job and volunteers at the shelter. We hardly ever go out together," Christian complained.

"How boring! Life should be about being happy and having fun," the Zumba girl moaned. "I don't like people who are so serious all the time."

"And she won't let me eat any meat. I have to sneak out of the house just to have a burger or a steak," he groaned.

Since when was this a problem?

I thought he agreed to eat only vegan food at home because he cared about the animals.

"Oh, no! That's just crazy. It's your house, and you are a man; you should be setting the rules."

"I know, but she insisted. It was important to her, so I thought I'd give it a try. A plant-based meal plan. Many people swear by that."

"It's just a fad. How can you build muscle if you don't eat your protein? A man needs his protein, especially a big, sexy man like you," she moaned in response. "I like meat, umm, hmmm..."

I just stood there, contemplating my next move. All that groaning and moaning made me think they were making out or maybe even having sex. What a dick! I thought.

Meanwhile, Mr. Dick, a.k.a. Christian Fox, which was his real name, didn't expect me to be home at that time. I was only there because I forgot my laptop and pen drive with documents, which I needed for the meeting I was planning to attend later that day at the city hall about children's and senior's programs the city was planning to start in the fall. Children and seniors interacting with the animals from the shelter would be great for both children and animals. The whole presentation and other files were on my laptop. Both of which were sitting on the night table next to the bed.

"She won't let me bring any cheese or sausage into the house. There's nothing for me to eat in the refrigerator. I go to bed hungry on most nights since she moved in," he said. "And in the morning, she makes me juices and smoothies, no eggs and bacon."

"Oh, poor Christian! That's not a way to treat a man. Making him eat rabbit food," she squealed. "Besides, juicing is so wasteful. Those vegan punks throw away tons of perfectly edible food."

"I have to eat tofu and fake meats. And drink soy beverage instead of real milk," he moaned.

"You have to be careful with soy. It's not good for a man," she moaned back. "I'm not sure exactly why, but something about the hormones. I don't eat soy. Ever."

"Yeah, I heard about it too. When she makes something with soy, I pretend to eat it, but make sure I spit it out."

My mouth practically fell open.

Secretly spitting out food, like a kindergartner? What is he—five?

"How come you two are even together? You seem so different, so… incompatible. She sounds like a real bitch."

"When I met her, she didn't have a place to live. She was so miserable; I thought if I'd help her, it'll cheer her up. So I suggested that she moved in with me and let her stay in my place till she found an apartment of her own."

"And that's her gratitude? Trying to convert you to some fad diet? My poor Christian!" she gushes.

So he only was with me out of pity? How interesting! What else was I going to find out?

I keep listening as my 'poor Christian' continues. "She cooks beans all the time! They make me gassy like you wouldn't believe."

"Uh, hmm," she growled. "I don't believe in beans. They are so not Paleo."

"Yeah, me neither. I love eating like a caveman; that's the way to go. All-natural, no fake meats or other foods," he grunted. "Uh-huh… Oh, Anastasia, this was the best idea ever," he said with a loud sigh. "We should do it more often."

"With pleasure, Christian," she purred. "We can do it any time you want."

So the Zumba girl's name was Anastasia?

"Oh, my… yeah, like a caveman and a cavewoman," she moaned. "It's so sensual and … sexy. Oh, Christian, you're so sexy."

'Oh my?' Who did she think she was? Anastasia freaking Steele? Then I realized the coincidence: Anastasia and Christian, go figure. Just like in the Fifty Shades of Grey. I almost burst out laughing. Was Ana's inner goddess dancing Zumba with Mr. Christian Grey on my bed?

"You are so sexy yourself," Mr. Christian Grey said slowly in a husky voice.

He never talked in a husky voice to me.

What were they doing in there, anyway? I wondered. And what was that smell? I hadn't noticed it before. Strong and repugnant. It reminded me of something that I couldn't quite place.

It didn't sound like they were having sex, but I couldn't see for sure without opening the doors wider, which might startle them. The door had been squeaking for weeks. I asked Christian to do something about it, but he kept forgetting. Funny how he never forgot to wax his sports car. Even the wheels were always spotless and shining.

I glanced at my watch. I needed to get moving. What I didn't need was listen to this Zumba expert lecture on nutrition. And yet, I felt perversely captivated by the spying experience. It was something I expected sooner or later to happen. It always did.

After all, men are cheaters; that's the universal truth.

I braced myself before I entered the room, not sure what I'd see. Were they naked? On my sheets? I reached for the door but stopped as the conversation continued.

"She even feeds her dogs mostly vegan food," Christian says.

"No! Really? You should report her to animal services," she says. "She certainly sounds like a freak. Did you hear that they feed animals with dog meat at that shelter of hers?"

I gasped in disbelief. What on earth was she talking about?

There's a pause. "That can't be true," Christian said.

"Totally. It was on the news. They're investigating a chain of restaurants, Bamboo Palace, or something like that. Chinese places. Someone got poisoned with salmonella, and they found meat that looked suspicious."

That was all that I could bear.

How dare she say things like that about me and the shelter!

And Christian? He never complained about my food. Or said that he wanted to go out more. Most nights, he preferred just lazing on the sofa watching the sports channel after he was back from the gym.

Lying, cheating, two-faced bastard. Just like the rest of them!

I opened the door wide and made a dramatic entrance into the room.

***

I strode into the center of the bedroom, tripping over the shoes and

19

pieces of clothing scattered on the floor. When I regained my balance and composure, I looked at the two love birds, trying to understand what was happening.

Christian and the Zumba girl were lounging on my bed, almost fully dressed, except for their shoes, with a large tray in the middle of the bed, filled with takeout boxes and napkins with a familiar logo.

So all that moaning and groaning made me suspect that they were having sex, when, in fact, they were eating giant juicy hamburgers and chicken wings from the Best Fried Chicken, the fast-food joint just around the corner from the Big and Strong Gym.

I used to frequent that place in my former life but stopped after I became vegan because, except for fries and ketchup, there was nothing for me to eat there. And even if there was, all the smells of the fried body parts of birds and pigs made me queasy.

Christian didn't seem to have a problem with us agreeing to eat only vegan food at home until today. Obviously, it all had been an act.

Looking at them, sitting on the bed, their mouths hanging open, I couldn't tell whether they were before or after sex. Or maybe that was it—they were having an orgy in the bedroom—only with food.

It wasn't what I expected to see. I was outraged and felt humiliated, but instead of screaming, I almost burst out laughing.

"Sorry to interrupt. Don't mind me. I just need to get my laptop," I said, trying to keep my composure. There would be time for rage and humiliation, maybe even tears, but at that moment, I needed to keep my cool.

Christian jumped up when he saw me, spilling ketchup and French fries all over my sheets. "Olivia, please, let me explain," he mumbled. He finally found his voice after the awkward moment when both of them were too flabbergasted to say anything.

"Please… don't go… Olivia!"

"We were not doing anything. Just having a bite to eat," the Zumba girl chimed in. "It's not what you think."

"Oh? And how do you know what I think?" I asked. To me, the fact that they weren't having sex wasn't any better; it was worse.

The fact that he brought someone into our bedroom was terrible. But laughing about me behind my back? Making jokes about my ethical choices? Mocking me with another woman? Just like my father did about my mom. It was even worse than him having sex with her.

"Can we talk about it like grownups?" he asked.

"We'll talk tonight."

"Just let me explain," he insisted.

"I'm already late for the meeting," I said, gathering my stuff for the presentation.

Where is that damn pen drive? I thought as I rummaged through the drawers of the bedside table.

"Then let's talk about it tonight, over dinner," he said. "I'll cook something special for you."

"Don't." I turned to him and added, "I'll take care of the food, and we'll talk. And bring the dogs back into the apartment before you leave," I said as I ran out. He wanted to follow me, but I slammed the door in his face before he could tell me another lie.

It was over—this time for good. I wasn't going to end up like my mother.

I just wanted us to have one last meal together before moving out, and I already had a plan.

6.

Just great. I was broke, jobless, and now—without a boyfriend or a place to live. I had no money for a down-payment because I donated pretty much everything to the shelter and other charitable organizations.

From the apartment, I went straight to the city council meeting. It was a favor for Patricia, an old friend from law school. She was doing some pro-bono work and couldn't attend the meeting herself. They were going to discuss some new bills, and I was supposed to take notes for her. I turned on the audio recorder on my phone, as I couldn't concentrate on the discussion and had no idea what it was about. I kept going back to what had happened, analyzing every word, trying to figure out what to do next.

Breaking up with Christian sounded like an obvious thing to do. The problem was I had to move out but had no place to go. Ever since I quit my job as a lawyer, I had no money to rent my own place. I tried to find a job that would pay the bills, but it wasn't as easy as I hoped it would be. I didn't want to work for peanuts, and that's what most positions that were close to home and the shelter offered. Thankfully, I had some savings, but those were running out fast. They weren't going to last if I didn't have a regular income, and no bank would give me credit with no steady job and thousands of dollars in college debt.

I needed to think.

And vent some of that steam before tonight.

I decided to go to the gym, get a workout, and a shower. My membership was going to expire soon, so I might as well use it.

The bag with gym clothes was in my trunk all the time, which made such last-minute decisions easy. As I was changing into my baggy pants and a t-shirt, I kept thinking about my situation.

The law school was a giant money pit. My parents talked me into it, and I agreed. I had to finish something. Get a degree. A good education was essential. Since I was a little girl, I wanted to be a lawyer, just like my daddy. To argue in court in defense of innocent individuals unjustly accused of wrongdoing. Of course, later on, things changed between my father and me, he stopped being my hero, but somehow I didn't know what else I could do. For a while, I thought about becoming a veterinarian, but I'm too squeamish about being a doctor (the sight of blood and wounds makes me nauseous), so I went through the motions of getting through law school.

The problem was it put me deeply in debt. With my father mostly cutting us off after the divorce and my mom having trouble finding and keeping a steady job, we were poor. My dad promised me that if I'd go to law school, he'd help me pay for it but ended up paying for only half of it. He claimed that his situation had changed and couldn't afford it anymore. Of course, he had plenty of money; it just wasn't his. He married a daughter of a very successful businessman. Besides, I needed to get back on my feet and earn my way through school, he told me. Nobody ever gave him anything, and look how he turned out; he liked to say. He didn't want me to end up like those rich, entitled brats, who didn't appreciate real work.

After I graduated, I realized I didn't want to pursue a career in law. My friends were getting jobs, on track to becoming partners, while I was getting nowhere. I applied to a couple of firms and even got accepted, but my heart just wasn't in it. It became evident that just as often as arguing to save innocent people, I'd be getting suspicious individuals off the hook.

I also realized that if I wanted to do something for the animals, then getting into law wasn't the best option. The more I looked into the animal legislation, the more apparent it became to me that law wasn't on the side of the animals. As far as animal rights, the law was part of the problem, not part of the solution.

For one thing, the law stated that animals were property, and therefore humans had infinite power over them. The so-called welfare laws were a joke, protecting only certain species and only to some extent. Farm animals, i.e., the vast majority of animals that exist today, don't have any protection whatsoever. They're treated as property, mere objects, or a means to an end.

The animal laws attorneys dealt mostly with custody disputes over animals when couples were separating or getting divorced or veterinary malpractice suits. Those cases had nothing to do with protecting animals from abuse.

I realized there was little I could do for the animals when working in a comfortable law office.

So I decided to find a rescue organization or an animal sanctuary, and that's how I ended up in the Kind Heart Animal shelter. Then I met Christian, who worked as a personal trainer at the local gym. I never hired him to train me, but he gave me tips on how to use weights and machines, and we somehow ended up living together after a couple of months into my gym membership.

I didn't have a place to stay when my previous landlord kicked me out (neighbors were complaining about dogs being too loud, he told me), and Christian suggested that I could move in with him. My grandmother suggested that I ask my father for help, but I didn't want to do that. Christian and I ended up living together in a sort of relationship that was going nowhere, at least as far as I was concerned. We never really talked about the future, but the fact that we were sleeping together surely meant something. He let me bring my dogs and even agreed that we only kept vegan food in the house, which was nice of him.

Did that mean that I was using him or trying to convert him by force? It was not how I saw it. He seemed to care about me, understand my concern about the animals, and was okay with the changes that I suggested—remembering all that made me feel even angrier.

And now what?

I didn't know where to go since my current home wasn't my home anymore. Penelope would be the obvious choice, but she had a new boyfriend. Eric, on the other hand, lived alone, so I decided to ask him.

I took out my phone and texted him discretely.

Me: 'I need a place to stay for a few nights. It's an emergency.'

Eric wrote me right back: 'Did you break up with Christian???' His text was followed with a row of emojis showing faces in distress.

Is he a mind reader? Either that, or he knew me far too well.

Me: 'Yes.'

Him: 'You know where to find the key. C U home tonight :-)', followed by a row of hearts and kisses.

"Thanks!' I wrote back.

There were just two things that I wanted to do before I ended my relationship with Christian.

I needed to pack my things and prepare the 'last supper,'

It would be the last meal I had with Christian, and I wanted to make it special.

7.

I delayed going home, even though I was sure that neither Christian nor the Zumba girl would be there any longer. The fact that I had to talk to Christian made me feel even more drained. What was I going to tell him? There was really nothing to say.

I didn't want to relive those moments or have to look at the mess—the evidence of their passionate meal and his betrayal—but I had no choice. The sooner I'd be done with it, the better.

It turned out, at the very least, they had the decency to clean up after themselves. Christian wasn't very neat and organized, but he even changed the sheets and put the ones they used in the laundry. It was kind of him, although he didn't have to do it. It wasn't like that would get him any brownie points. I noticed that he put on my favorite set—animal print, with birds, butterflies, and flowers. It had lovely colors that always cheered me up in the morning. But not this time. I needed to get out of his apartment, and the sooner, the better. I packed my things and carried them to my car.

I opened the refrigerator and considered my options. I was hungry but didn't feel like cooking. I remembered what Christian had said, that there was never anything for him to eat there.

I disagreed.

The refrigerator was full of food.

To be fair, (I had to admit looking at the content), it wasn't your typical all-American fridge. The top was filled with various colorful fruits and vegetables, the bottom with leafy greens. The middle and the door shelves were stacked with plant milks, hummus, a few packets of tofu, containers with cooked beans, and grains—no typical fare, such as egg, meat, or dairy cheeses.

I thought about making a vegetable juice but then remembered what the Zumba girl said about juicing being wasteful. The truth was I felt bad about throwing away the pulp that was left after juicing, even though I knew it was going into the compost pile and back into the earth. There must be a better way to use it. I wondered what the zero waste people would say about it; I'd have to look into that sometime.

Meanwhile, I took my blender and started filling it with greens for a smoothie—a mix of kale, collard greens, and spinach, followed with a couple of bananas and a pint of strawberries. I didn't bother to remove the leaves. I added a cup of water and turned the engine to the highest setting. After about ten seconds, I switched it off, took out an oversized beer glass, poured the green mixture, and took a sip.

So, I'm not the world's greatest chef, but I do know how to make a green smoothie that tastes better than a five-course meal at the poshest restaurant in town.

As I gulped it down slowly, I felt my body filling with goodness. Unwittingly, I let out a moan, "Oh, my. Yummm."

Wait, did I sound like the Zumba girl, who, in turn, sounded like Anastasia Steele in the freaking Fifty Shades of Gray?

I snorted, almost choking on a piece of fruit that didn't get blended. Maybe. Probably. So what?

Anastasia and Christian had already proven that food could be a potent aphrodisiac. And, in some cases, maybe even better than sex.

8.

I QUICKLY SET THE TABLE AND MADE SURE THE FOOD WAS kept warm in the oven. I remembered my mother waiting for my father to come back from work, his late-night meetings with supporters, prominent people in business, and influential politicians.

Mom would prepare elaborate three-course dinners, but he wasn't even hungry. And when she asked about his day, he'd lie. He'd make up some story of why he was late, and my mother would believe him.

And even if she didn't, she wouldn't question him. She never made a scene. Never cried or shouted. Never said an angry word.

But I'm not my mother.

For one, instead of cooking at home, I ordered takeout. And for the other, I was going to break with Christian and tell him I was moving out immediately.

"Uhmmm. It smells yummy-licious," Christian murmured as he entered the kitchen.

Was that the husky voice I heard earlier today? *Don't you try your Mr. Grey's tactics on me,* I thought and said, "I ordered some food for dinner."

"I thought you'd prefer to go out," he said.

"I'm tired and want to stay in. You don't mind, do you?"

"Not at all. There's a game on Channel 23 at seven. Maybe we could watch some."

"Sure," I said. I put food on two plates and placed them on the table, one in front of Christian, the other in front of me.

"Look, I'm sorry about what happened. It didn't mean anything," Christian started.

"So, what else did you do today? Anything exciting?" I cut him off. He seemed taken aback. He expected a fight or an argument, but I was calm as if nothing had happened. I knew how to do that well; I'd seen my mom do it many times when my father came home.

"Oh, nothing much. I had a few private training sessions, the usual stuff. What's that?" he asked, poking his food suspiciously with a chopstick.

"Chicken."

"You ordered chicken for me? That's a first," he says, surprised. When I moved in, I made it clear that I didn't want any dead animals in the house.

"Yes, don't you like chicken?" I asked.

"I do," he said cautiously. "I just thought… Never mind. Thanks. He put a slice in his mouth. Uhm. It's good. Different, but good. Where did you get it?"

"There's this new Chinese place that I wanted to try. Bamboo Palace or something. It's a new chain in town."

"Chinese?" He stopped chewing. "Didn't you hear what they say?"

"What?" I asked innocently.

"There are rumors."

"What rumors?"

"About the meat, they're serving."

"Oh, the dog meat rumor," I laughed, but my laughter sounded ominous, not cheerful. "You don't believe that, do you?"

"No, I don't. I mean, I don't know." He resumed chewing. His forehead was all wrinkled as if he was thinking intensely.

Poor Christian, I could almost hear the wheels spinning in his head as he was trying to figure out what to say. He is good looking and very fit, but his intellect isn't his forte.

"Are you sure this is a reputable place?" he finally asked. "Have you checked the reviews? What's this dish even called? Are you sure this is real chicken?"

"You mean the one that has feathers and wings, and feels pain when they hang them upside down before they cut its throat and let it bleed to death?" I said and shook my head. "No. I don't think that's that kind of chicken. But it looks good."

He looked at me, disgusted.

"They didn't have a menu in English, just Chinese, with pictures alongside the dishes. I asked them to recommend something for a chicken lover. I just looked at the pictures on the menu to order."

"So you don't even know what this is?" he spat out chunks of food back on his plate. "It could be… anything."

"Even if that's dog meat, which I assure you it's not, what's the difference?" I asked, battling my eyelashes innocently.

"What do you mean? Of course, it makes a difference," he said with anger. "Why are you talking like that to me? You're acting weird. Are you angry with me or something?"

I crossed my arms on my chest. "Yeah, something."

"Is it about what happened today, because if it is—"

"Okay. You're right. It's about you and that Zumba bimbo having fun in our bedroom today."

"I told you it was nothing. And Anastasia is not a bimbo. You should have joined us and have some fries with ketchup or something. She's really nice."

"Sorry I couldn't join the party. Maybe another time. Besides, I didn't want to intrude on your private training session," I said with sarcasm.

"We were just having lunch. We didn't do anything, I swear. We didn't have sex if that's what bothers you. We just had a bite to eat."

"And you think that's nothing? Ordering from Big Freaking Chicken and laughing about me behind my back," I hissed.

"Oh, so that's what this is about? It's just about the food?"

"No, Christian. It's not *just about the food*. It's about you being a liar and a cheater."

"Okay, fine. You're such a self-righteous…" he paused and hesitated.

"I'm such a self-righteous what?"

"Never mind. I'm not going to finish that chicken."

"You don't have to," I said. "But don't worry. It's not dog's meat. It comes from the Bamboo Veggie Garden; I just remembered the name. It's one hundred percent vegan, so you didn't eat a dog or a chicken. So relax. It's plant-based meat."

Christian rolled his eyes. "You know what your problem is, Olivia?

You don't care about people. All you care about is those cats, dogs, cows, and chickens. Did you ever even care about me?"

I ignored the question and started getting ready to leave.

"Yeah, that's what I thought."

"I think I better go now. The dogs won't bother you anymore. And neither will my strange eating habits," I said.

It was weird how calm I was. I should be more upset. Crying, screaming, making a scene. Maybe there is something wrong with me and my emotions. Maybe I'm a little bit like my mother, after all.

Another one bites the dust; I sighed as I drove off.

Why do those things always happen to me?

Why don't they happen to somebody else?

Not that I'd wish that on anybody. But why me—again?

Never again! I'm done with men, I promised myself. It was six months ago. And I was going to keep my promise, no matter what.

So when Ryan Kowalski entered the office, or what was left of it, I had no intention to succumb to his charm.

9.

After making sure that the cats are okay, I go back to the office. I'm curious about what's going on in there. I'm kind of hoping that the fireman is still there. And he is.

Everyone except Penelope and Maria is gone.

"Are you sure you want Ruffy? He may not be ready for adoption. He needs someone who'll know how to handle him," I hear Penelope say. "Olivia is in charge of adoptions. She'll explain everything."

Her phone rings and she steps out to answer the call.

Ryan turns to me.

He wants to adopt Ruffy? Why?

"He came from a puppy mill, which means he may be messed up for life," I say.

Ryan shrugs. "I wouldn't worry about that. I'm great with dogs. They just love me," he says and smiles disarmingly, making Maria, the new volunteer, giggle. Oh my goodness, he's so full of himself. He must know what effect he has on women, no doubt about it.

"The previous owner complained about him being a pain in the neck. Barking, biting, destroying things around the house," I continue.

"Well, what did they expect? It's a dog," he chuckles. "If they wanted something soft and cuddly, they should have gotten a plush toy. Right? Seriously, I don't mind. Like I'm saying, I have experience with dogs, and I think he likes me too."

"You realize that we still have to vet you and that once you're approved and take him home, you won't be able to change your mind and return him."

"Of course!" He scoffs. "I have no intention of doing that. So how long is the procedure, and what should I do?"

"It takes several weeks to a couple of months. You have to visit the dog several times to interact with him. Then, depending on how you do, we'll review your application and give you our decision."

He opens his eyes wide. "You can't be serious. I thought you wanted people to adopt, especially after what happened."

"We have to make sure the animals are in good hands. We can't just give them to anybody."

"I'm not just anybody," he stares at me intensely, piercing me with his blue eyes.

"You know what I mean," I mumble. Maybe I didn't say it right, but who does he think he is, anyway? "It will give you time to think over your decision as well."

He keeps staring at me, which makes me feel self-conscious. I bite my lip. *Am I blushing? Stop it, Olivia!*

"There's nothing to think about. I know I want that dog, and if he has issues, he shouldn't spend another day here. He should be home where someone can take care of him," he says with that smug expression on his face that's so irritating.

Why does he want that dog so badly?

"Have you considered other dogs?" I ask. "It might take less time if—"

"No. I want him, and that's it. I feel we're meant for each other," he interrupts me. His phone beeps and he reaches into his pocket. He glances at the display and frowns. "I have to go now, but I'll be back to see how Ruffy is doing. We can talk more about this then."

I shoot him an annoyed look. "Well, maybe. But we already have someone interested in him."

"Is that so?" Ryan raises his eyebrows. "I'm not seeing people flocking to adopt your cats and dogs." He takes a look around, rotating his head slowly for dramatic effect. He really is super annoying. "I'm the one who saved you, and I'm the one he trusts."

I roll my eyes. "Yeah, so? Maybe you're not the right fit," I hiss, irritated by his over-confidence. "Look, what you did is admirable, but the coverage was a little bit over the top, don't you think?"

He looks at me, taken aback. I bet he isn't used to such treatment.

"How do you mean?" he asks.

"I mean—" I hesitate. "You were all over the front pages and second pages, and all over the Internet, and it's great, But the fact is no one cares what happens to those animals after they've been saved."

He keeps staring at me, his blue eyes open wide, so I continue. "Plus, if you aren't vegan, then you contribute to the suffering and violent death of hundreds of animals for your pleasure and amusement. And that's not okay," I gush.

Finally, Ryan blinks and asks, "Isn't that a matter of personal choice what a person eats? Aren't vegans a bit self-righteous wanting to judge everybody based on their way of living and eating?"

I cross my arms on my chest and frown. "The color of your car is a personal choice; torturing and killing another being, it's not."

Maria looks up at me from her computer in shock, and I just shrug.

"Fine. Suit yourself. No wonder you're having problems placing these animals in good homes," he says when he's already in the door.

As Ryan is leaving, Barbara and Eric return. Barbara looks after Ryan and asks, "Is that Ryan Kowalski? What did he want?"

"He asked about Ruffy and said he wanted to adopt him," I reply.

"He wants to adopt Ruffy? That's wonderful!" Barbara says with glee. "Did you tell him about his issues?"

"Of course."

"He said he couldn't leave him in the shelter to die. Not after he risked his life to save him," Maria says, looking at me with reproach. I shrug and ignore her stare.

Barbara claps her hands. "I'm so happy Ruffy will have a home."

"Only, I'm not sure if he'll be back because Olivia practically chased him away, scaring him of our adoption procedure," Maria says.

"You did what?" Barbara looks at me, appalled.

I frown. "We still have to vet him. Hero or not, he must go through the whole procedure, just like everybody else," I explain.

The truth was the first owners returned him because he was so ill-behaved. The second said they couldn't take care of him any longer because they had to sell their house, and the apartment they had to move into didn't accept dogs. Then they admitted that the dog was a pain in the neck; he barked and bit them and didn't like to be cuddled. It was something they didn't expect, even though we warned them that he needed special care. And with the third—there were rumors that they were abusing him, so animal services had to step in, and now Ruffy's back where he started.

Barbara nods. "Well, that's something that we need to discuss. Maybe we're too strict."

I look at her, alarmed. "What are you saying? That we should be less rigid? Accept anyone who just wants a pet? Such an irresponsible attitude would do more harm than good."

Barbara sighs heavily. "We're running out of space. People keep bringing us animals, but where are we going to put them all? Who's going to pay for their food and medicines? We're well past our capacity, and we don't have any money left. Insurance will only cover so much."

"Maybe I'll adopt him," I blurt out.

Barbara shakes her head. "You can't adopt every dog that has issues. Especially since you already have three. You can't save them all."

She's right. I'm already having problems finding a place to live, but another dog won't make a big difference. "I'm just saying that we shouldn't rush through the adoption process. We should be careful not to make a mistake," I insist.

"And I'm saying that maybe we shouldn't be as rigid," Barbara retorts. "If someone comes to us and tells us that they want to adopt, then we should make it super easy for them, especially if it's someone respectable. Someone who has what it takes and really wants to help."

I shrug. "Yeah, sure. Everybody says so, and then the dog is back before you know it. Most people can't be trusted," I mutter. I finish my coffee and get up. "I'll check on Ruffy and see how he's doing."

Barbara raises her hand. "Wait. Before you go, I have something to tell you," she says.

10.

"WE MAY HAVE TO CLOSE DOWN THE SHELTER," Barbara announces, once she has our full attention. "As most of you already know, we don't have the money to rebuild the facilities while caring for all these animals. We need to schedule a meeting of the shelter employees and volunteers so I can tell everybody the news."

"What? When?" We look at each other in shock.

I knew the Kind Heart Animal shelter was struggling, but closing?

That was never an option!

At least that's what I thought.

"The building is a total mess, and we're running off supplies. Some animals are still recovering and need medical attention. I know you're doing your best, and I'm grateful to all of you, but we must face the truth," Barbara says.

"Don't we have insurance?" Eric asks.

"The shelter was insured, and we're planning to rebuild, but we may not get enough. There are rumors that we set the fire ourselves to get the money, and that's insurance fraud."

"That's outrageous!"

"The investigation may take weeks or months, and we just don't have the time. In the meantime, the donations are barely enough to provide treatment for the affected animals, transportation of animals in need of relocation, and replacements for the veterinary supplies that went up in smoke."

I shake my head. "What will happen to the animals if we close?"

"We'll have to move them to other shelters," Barbara says.

"But who will take them? All shelters are overcrowded, and they have to euthanize the animals to make room for new ones," I say. "Meanwhile, the breeders are happily breeding new cats and dogs, selling them online and through the pet stores, making loads of money, and laughing all the way to the bank. They don't care what happens to those animals later. When, in fact, they should be the ones responsible for paying for their care. They are breeding them faster than we can save them. The whole system is a disgrace."

Barbara sighs and slumps heavily on the chair.

"We cannot just close down like that!" I say. "There must be something we can do."

"We're out of money, Olivia, and that's the truth. I don't even know if we can make it till the end of this year," Barbara says grimly.

"We can get more donations," Eric suggests. "Or find new sponsors. Surely we can find someone who'll help us."

"Donations? From whom?" Barbara asks. "Besides, the donations that we've been getting from people are just not enough."

"So we must get more creative. Get new sponsors. Maybe set up a campaign online. People want to help, but you have to ask them. I'll look into that," Penelope offers.

"This is so frustrating. Why do we even have to keep asking?" I say bitterly. "We're trying to convince people to do the right thing by supporting the homeless animals. Meanwhile, the breeders and pet shops are doing great, breeding and selling animals, creating the very problem we have to deal with. Truth is we're cleaning up their messes, but people don't care. Everybody only thinks about themselves."

The room falls silent.

"You don't understand; people have mortgages, kids in college, bills to pay," Barbara replies. "You're young and with no family obligations."

"Right, so who cares what happens to some homeless dogs and cats? It's not their problem, is that what you mean?" I snarl. I know I'm not being fair. Barbara is the oldest in our group; her kids grown up and gone, she devotes her whole heart to this place. She's the last person I should be shouting at, and yet, I can't help but vent my frustration at her.

"Surely, that's not true. What about those firemen and everybody else who's been helping us in the past few days?" Penelope says. "This means people do care."

"Oh, yeah, let's not forget about Ryan Kowalski, who risked his life to save those animals! Saving dogs and cats from a burning building!" I sneer. "And now thousands of people are watching him on television and sharing the story on social media." I put my hands on my hips and continue, "Sure, people like to watch that kind of thing. And then they pat themselves on the back, thinking, oh, look, if it weren't for humans, that poor creature would perish. When the truth is—if it weren't for humans, that creature wouldn't need to be rescued. All these animals wouldn't be in that situation in the first place. We, humans, are the problem. And I'm not just talking about that poor dog, but billions of animals tortured and killed every year for food and entertainment."

"Olivia, you're not helping," Penelope interrupts me and turns to Barbara, "Don't we have any other options?"

Barbara spreads her arms in a gesture of hopelessness. "I looked into everything, and I don't see how we can continue. We need money to run the shelter. Food, medications, paying the vets—it adds up. And money is something that we just don't have."

Penelope keeps chewing on her pen intently, which she does when she is thinking hard. It's a habit that makes all the pens and pencils in the shelter look disgusting.

"Stop it," I say with frustration.

Suddenly Penelope jumps up and says, "Maybe there is something we can do." Her brain seems to be in overdrive as she keeps on chewing.

We all look at her expectantly, waiting to hear the genius idea.

"But first, Olivia will have to apologize to Ryan and help him with the adoption process," she says.

I turn to her, surprised.

"What? No way!" I gasp.

"Way! I heard about what happened, and you need to fix it. Do you want to save the shelter or not?"

I nod. Of course, I do.

But why should I be the one apologizing?

What kind of plan is that?

11.

"SO, WHAT DO YOU SUGGEST THAT WE DO?" Barbara asks after a moment of silence. "I'd be interested to hear any ideas that make sense."

"One thing we can do, we should make our adoption process easier," Eric says. "If more people can adopt, we'd have fewer animals to take care of."

Barbara nods. "I've been thinking about it myself."

"How do you mean?" I ask.

"If we find more homes for animals, then we won't need so many kennels, as well as less food, fewer supplies, and fewer employees," Barbara explains. "But to do that, we need to change our adoption process to make it less strict. I look through the applications—" she pauses and looks at me sternly. "We're rejecting people who are perfectly suitable to adopt."

"Sending people like Ryan away is unacceptable," Eric says.

I shrug. "I simply told him that he had to go through the extended procedure because the dog he wants to adopt has issues. We can't just accept anybody."

Barbara sighs. "I've looked through the application forms lately, and some of the requirements are just ridiculous. And unrealistic. Nobody can live up to those standards. No wonder our adoption rate is so low."

"So, what are you saying?" I ask.

"I'm saying that we should intensify our outreach to the community to find more forever homes for our dogs and cats."

"And we should use someone else's attention to get what we want. Capitalize on it." Penelope chimes in.

Barbara turns to her. "I don't understand."

"Me neither," I say. "Can you be a little more specific?"

"Sure." Penelope smiles. "We should have a fundraiser that engages the whole community—adoption and fundraising in one.”

"We did a bake sale last month, remember?" I interrupt, "and the money we made barely covered the cost of renting the equipment and purchasing the ingredients."

Penelope rolls her eyes at me and gives me a condescending look.

"Trust me; I know all this. Except, this time, it will be different. We'll get someone to help us. Someone famous and trustworthy—" She pauses as her phone plays a happy tune. "I must answer this call real quick," she says and runs out of the room to take the call.

Barbara turns to me with a frown.

I shrug. "Don't ask me." I'm used to surprises from Penelope but have no clue of what she's up to this time.

12.

"I KNOW WHO WILL HELP US WITH THE FUNDRAISER!" Penelope announces when she returns to the office and waits for our reactions.

"Well? Are you going to tell us?" I'm still annoyed at her for her wanting me to apologize to that firefighter guy.

She points to the newspaper on Barbara's desk. "That guy."

"What guy? I don't get it," Barbara says.

"OMG! That's Ryan Kowalski. That's him on the front page!" Maria shrieks.

"Duh," I mumble.

The front page of the Herald Tribune, the local paper, features a big photo of a firefighter holding a dog with a burning building in the background. The same man I practically threw out of the office just hours ago. Suddenly, I understand Penelope's wicked plan.

"No!" I object.

"Yes!" Penelope smiles cheerfully. "Ryan Kowalski, that's whom."

Ryan Kowalski, in the photo, has a big smile on his face. He's obviously proud of himself. And full of himself, too. He sure looks like that type to me.

The truth is, all men look like that to me. I can't pinpoint the time when I first started to distrust men, but the latest disaster with Christian wasn't the first, and probably not the last one either. For that reason, I prefer the company of dogs and cats. At least they don't lie to my face and pretend that they love me, when if fact, they're having sex with someone else.

"That guy? Really?" I ask, acting like I'm still not understanding what Penelope has in mind.

Penelope nods. "Exactly. The firefighter who risked his life to rescue a dog—everybody is talking about him. Ryan Schwarzenegger. The

41

Hero. He'll be the perfect picture boy for our campaign and fundraiser."

"Wait. His name is Schwarzenegger?" Maria asks, looking confused.

"Of course not. He's much better looking than Arnold. Not to mention younger. With beautiful eyes…" Penelope says in a dreamy voice. I'm not sure if she is being serious or testing our patience. "But that's not my point. The point is that people recognize him. He is famous, even if for a brief moment, and we could use it for our cause."

"That's your big idea?" I ask skeptically.

After the way I treated him, I doubt it could work.

"Ryan Kowalski will be our bait. Attraction. Money-magnet. Whatever you call him. He'll be the face of our new campaign."

"It's brilliant." Eric claps his hands.

Barbara nods thoughtfully. "It could work."

Ryan Kowalski is never coming back here; I want to yell but don't.

"And he'll help us because—?" I ask.

"He's a nice guy," Eric says.

I roll my eyes. "How do you know that?" The fact that Eric has a crush on Ryan doesn't make him objective.

"Because he saved Ruffy's life. And not just Ruffy's, he saved many animals that night," Penelope chimes in. "And because I've already set up a meeting with him. The meeting is in two hours at the fire station." Penelope slumps down on her chair, obviously proud of herself.

"Okay, good luck, then," I mumble.

"Unfortunately, as much as I'd like to go, I can't. Besides, since you need to apologize, it's best that you go, Olivia." Everyone looks at me.

"And you think that if I ask him to do a fundraiser with us, he'll agree?"

"He wants to adopt Ruffy, remember," Penelope replies. "Come on! Be a little bit more enthusiastic. Some positive energy is what we need right now," she says and winks at me. Then she leans forward and whispers in my ear, "It will be good for the shelter, and for you, too, if you're lucky."

Now it's my turn to do an eye-roll. "Stop trying to set me up," I whisper back.

"You don't even know if he's single and available," Eric says, who's eavesdropping on our exchange.

Penelope turns to Eric, "If you're hoping he's gay, he is not, I assure you."

"Okay, so, Olivia will go and talk to Ryan Kowalski. But what's your plan if he agrees?" Barbara asks.

"I have a couple of ideas; I can put together a plan. But one thing we could do is create a calendar," Penelope says.

I shake my head. "Who buys calendars in the middle of the summer?"

"That's a fantastic idea!" Eric jumps up. "Have you seen that calendar of those Australian firefighters? So hot and muscular! I'm getting dizzy just thinking about it. Each of them looks like Adonis or Apollo."

Okay, so Ryan is quite good looking. But the rest of those guys?

I raise my hand. "Um, I don't know. They don't look like they're in the best shape. Too much pizza and barbecue ribs, probably. I don't know if that's what we're after."

"We're not doing a nude calendar, and they'll look super cute in their firefighters' outfits with our dogs and cats," Penelope declares. "Have you seen the movie Calendar Girls? Or the one about calendar boys, I don't recall the title. Anyway, that's what we could do—a calendar of firefighters and dogs and cats, with Ryan and Ruffy on the front page," Penelope keeps talking, all excited. "Have them pose for pictures with our animals. Let them play together, take them for a walk, or whatever, and have the photographer take photos. We want pictures that look natural, not staged."

Barbara nods. "That could work."

"We could set up an online store and upload our designs so that people can buy those things at any time. A print-on-demand service won't cost us a thing. All we need is a good photographer and graphic designer to put it all together. We could sell t-shirts, mugs, and other gadgets." Penelope gets up. "I have phone calls to make. Olivia, you need to leave now; Ryan is expecting you."

Eric jumps up from his seat. "I'll go with Olivia."

"She's a big girl," Barbara says. "Someone has to stay here,"

Penelope and I walk to our cars.

"He'll never agree to that," I say.

"Why not?"

Because he looks like a self-important jerk, who's full of himself, I want to say, but bite my lips.

Penelope pierces me with her eyes as if hearing what I'm thinking.

"Give him a chance, Olivia. You don't even know the guy."

"Maybe I don't know HIM, but I do know guys LIKE HIM. They can't be trusted. And they always have an agenda."

"Stop being so judgmental and cut people some slack. Besides, you're asking him to help us with a fundraiser, not marry you. We need money, and we need it fast. Right now, he's famous—practically a celebrity—even if just for a brief moment. It could work."

I have to agree; it's not a bad idea. Except I don't feel comfortable asking that guy for help. In fact, after the way I treated him, it's the last thing I want to do. "I…," I begin, trying to come up with an excuse, but Penelope looks at me crooked.

"You and your self-righteous, men-bashing comments. You have a problem; you realize that? Maybe you need therapy," she says. "Take anger management classes or something." Suddenly, she stops in the middle of the street and frowns.

"But you know what? This is not about you," she continues. "It's not about you screwing up your life. It's about the greater good. About the shelter and the animals that we must save."

A car honks at us loudly, and we run to the side of the street.

"Apologize and tell him that he can adopt Ruffy," she demands.

As much as I hate the idea, I know she's right. "Okay. I'll do it."

"Just try not to be so hostile. The shelter's future depends on it."

"No pressure, right?" I say sarcastically. "Don't worry; I can handle it," I add, even though I'm not so sure of it at all.

13.

THIS WHOLE DATING-LOVE-MARRIAGE THING ISN'T FOR ME. I have my passion. I have my soul-mates, the full shelter of them. A dog or a cat won't betray you. Animals won't cheat or lie or laugh about you behind your back. Penelope may laugh at me for saying that, but it's the truth. They depend on me completely, trust me, and love me unconditionally, just as much as I love them. They are giving me more love than I would ever get from any man.

Besides, I don't want to end up like my mother.

My father cheated on her for years. I knew about it, but I never said anything to either of my parents. My mom either didn't know about the affair or just preferred to act that way. I pretended that I didn't see it. But I knew. He couldn't fool me. I saw my dad and that other woman many times. They were more than just friends from work; I was sure of it.

My father may have suspected something because he gave me a dog for my tenth birthday. I loved that dog! Noelle was my favorite creature in the whole world. I liked her more than most of my friends at school, who were mean to me. I didn't have close friends back then, except Penelope.

Then, one night, Noelle disappeared. I thought that she got lost, so I searched for her for hours and hours. As the days went by, there was still no sign of Noelle. I put up posters and printed fliers.

I even offered a reward of one hundred sixteen dollars and fifty cents. It was all that I had saved from my allowance.

And then we had to sell the house. After the divorce, my mother and I rented a small two-bedroom apartment in a complex across town. My father moved into an elegant mansion, only now he had a new wife, the blond lady from the office, and a baby boy—my new brother.

It wasn't until months later that I learned what happened to Noelle. I overheard Grandma talking about it with my father. She said that giving the dog back to the shelter wasn't the right thing to do. But Dad said they weren't accepting pets in the apartment complex where we moved, and he couldn't take her either, as his new wife was allergic to dogs. So this was the best solution.

He just didn't want to bother and took her to a shelter.

Grandma tried to get the dog back, but Noelle was put to sleep. I begged Grandma to wake her, but she said it was too late. I didn't understand back then what it meant. Too late for what? I kept asking.

Of course, Noelle wasn't sleeping. She was dead.

That dog was my best friend. I loved her more than anybody else in the world—certainly more than my father, who was never around anyway. Always working, interested only in his career and his blond friend from the office.

So that night, I found Christian cheating—I made myself a promise. A pact that I wouldn't get into those relationships anymore and Penelope knew that.

I could still hear Eric's words in my head.

All those failed relationships. All those disasters, including the last one with Christian—were they my fault? Did I bring it all on myself?

Surely, Eric isn't blaming me for the fact that Christian cheated on me! Did I push him to do that? Into the embrace of the Zumba girl? How was it my fault that he almost had sex with her, wrapped in my sheets with pictures of me staring at them from the nightstand?

And my previous relationships? How was it my fault that they didn't work out? My former boyfriends were losers. Even if I wasn't entirely guilt-free, I didn't exactly push them away.

Or did I?

Are Eric and Penelope, right? Am I too rigid? The rules I follow, the high standards I'm trying to keep—they said nobody could live up to that, as if my must-have list of character traits was too extensive and unrealistic. But I expect no more of others than I demand of myself. It's only fair that I want a partner who shares my principles and values. Isn't it what genuine relationships are about?

Eric had no right to speak to me like that. And neither did

Penelope.

In fact, it was their fault, too. They insisted that I started dating again, even though I didn't want a romantic relationship in my life.

And now, too, I don't need a husky hero, who's probably full of himself and has women chasing him around town. I won't be one of them, no matter how many dogs he saves.

14.

So, I tried to come up with a better alternative for the fundraiser but couldn't. Plus, Penelope has her ways with people, so she finally convinced me to go along with her plan.

I decide to go there first thing in the morning. I drive up to the fire station and park my car. I find a spot in the shade and am just getting out of the car when I see a familiar figure leaving the station. Is that Anastasia, the Zumba girl?

Just great! I curse under my breath. It's the last person I wanted to see here. *What is she doing there anyway?*

Did she dump Christian and is dating firemen now?

I cross the street and enter the building.

"May I help you?" I hear a deep voice coming from behind a very red and shiny fire truck.

"Hello, I'm looking for Ryan Kowalski," I say.

"Then you found him!" the voice says. "And you are?"

"I came to talk about the dog."

"Oh. Penelope from the shelter?" the voice asks.

"No. I mean, yes. I mean, I'm from the shelter, but my name is Olivia Stone," I mumble. *What's happening to me?* I wonder.

"Oh, yes," the voice says.

"We met the other day when you came to talk about Ruffy—" I continue.

"Olivia, hi!" He finally appears from under the truck. "Please, come in." He points towards the room that looks like a kitchen and a lunchroom in one. "Penelope mentioned that you needed help with fundraising?" he says and smiles. I have to admit that he is good looking, but his pretty-boy charm won't work on me.

"Thank you for taking the time to talk to me," I say. "I wanted to apologize for my behavior the other day. I was completely out of line."

"Yes, you were," he says. "But it's not a big deal. I understand you have the good of the animals in mind."

I nod. "Of course, we'll be happy to work with you on Ruffy's adoption. Here, I brought you all the papers you need to fill out." I open my purse abruptly, and the sheets spill on the floor. "Sorry," I mumble. I get on my knees and start collecting them. "I'll be happy to assist you with the paperwork, of course," I add, embarrassed about my clumsiness.

Ryan kneels next to me and starts picking up the sheets with me.

"I'll be happy to give Ruffy a home. And help with the fundraising."

How charming, I think, wryly. But he won't fool me.

"Wow, that's a long application you have here. Am I supposed to fill all of these pages? It's going to take me the whole shift," he chuckles and starts polishing the front of the truck.

I shake my head and blow air on my bangs to get them out of my face. "Don't worry. I can help you with that," I say and continue, "Well, as Penelope may have explained, our shelter is in trouble. We need money, or our animals will have to be—" I hesitate.

"Killed," he finishes.

I nod. "We have till the end of the month to make the payment, or else the property will be auctioned and sold."

He looks at me with concern. "How much do you need?"

"About twenty thousand dollars."

He whistles. "That's a lot! We struggle to get donations, too."

I shake my head. "We aren't asking for money. We want you to help us organize a fundraising and adoption event."

He stops what he is doing, which is a relief. If he polishes that stainless steel thingy—whatever it is—any longer, it's going to turn into a mirror.

"Oh? How do you mean?" He looks at me and smiles. Or is that a smirk? Penelope was right; his eyes are beautiful. Why am I even paying attention to his eyes? That's not why I'm there. I almost blush. Gosh, I hope he didn't notice. Why do I always have to blush in the most inappropriate moments? It may give him the wrong idea. I suddenly feel self-conscious. As if those eyes could see deep inside me and read my thoughts.

"I'll have to talk to the rest of the team. We're just starting out running programs for children and seniors," he says.

"I understand," I nod. I had a feeling coming here was a bad idea, but still, I'm disappointed. Of course, the firefighters have their own agenda. Why should they help us?

"But I'm sure they'll agree to participate in your fundraiser," he adds, seeing my reaction. "So, what exactly do you have in mind?"

"Well," I begin, "we're thinking about doing a photo-shoot of you and other firefighters with our dogs and cats and then using those photos for creating items for sale. You know, cute t-shirts, mugs. Maybe even a calendar."

Ryan chuckles. "A calendar? Like those husky bare-chested firefighters from Australia did with their dogs?" He points to the wall behind him, where I notice precisely that—a calendar with bare-chested firefighters with dogs. "Are you asking us to pose bare-chested? I hope not because that would be indecent."

"No, of course not," I say, blushing. I curse Penelope for making me do this. She's so much better at convincing people to do things for her. Penelope could talk Eskimos into buying ice-cream; she's so persuasive.

"It won't be like that—just normal pictures. No nudity, I promise you," I gush. "This will be a family event. We want people to come and donate money and adopt. We'll bring our best-behaved dogs and cats so that people could adopt them if they like them," I keep talking, trying to avoid looking him in the eye, afraid that I'll blush.

What's happening to me? Surely, I'm not attracted to this guy. That's impossible!

I don't want to have anything to do with men, and that includes all men in uniforms, no matter how handsome they look or how husky their voices are.

"You'll let people adopt your dogs on the spot?" he asks.

"Well, maybe not on the spot, but we're working to speed up our procedures," I say.

"So how long will it take to process my application?"

If it were up to me, I wouldn't let him adopt. He's obviously a busy man. How will he be able to take care of a dog with serious issues like Ruffy? But others are fighting me on this. "You should be able to get the dog by the end of the week. The vet still wants to keep him for a few more days in case any other problems become evident. Come over whenever you can, and we'll go over the details."

"Okay, good. I'll stop by the shelter Friday morning, and we'll finalize the adoption," he says. "I should be able to talk to the team by then and give you our decision."

"Great," I say. "So, I'll see you on Friday. And we can talk about the photoshoot and fundraiser as well."

"Friday it is. It's a date," he says with that irritating expression on his face—is that supposed to be a smile? Because, to me, it seems like a smirk. A smug, self-satisfied smirk.

It's a date? Whatever.

I nod and stretch my lips in a smile.

Only why did he have to say it like that?

15.

The Kind Heart Animal shelter fundraiser date has been set for Sunday, the last weekend of May, which hopefully guarantees perfect weather. There is little time for preparations. We need to act fast and start planning immediately.

Penelope, who, in addition to working for the ad agency, also works part-time as a reporter for the local paper, commits to writing announcements and articles for the press. Eric will handle radio promotions, and I'll print fliers for posting on bulletin boards around town. Penelope's friend, Sylvia, a digital artist, and photographer will take pictures of firefighters and the event.

"This is outrageous!" Penelope exclaims all of a sudden.

"What?" I ask.

"Someone has been spreading rumors that we're feeding our animals dogs' meat," Penelope says. "The discussion is all over social media."

"What?"

"Who could say such a thing?"

"Doglover1277. They never sign their real names, of course."

"Just look at those nasty comments."

"We should respond and deny those allegations."

"You think those are not real comments?"

"How can they even think this is true? I wonder who's behind this."

"Look here—SweetAna16 says she's heard rumors that we've been feeding our dogs with dog meat, and Dogsrule50 says that we've been selling dog meat to Asian restaurants."

"But that is disgraceful!" I exclaim. "Nobody is going to believe that!"

"And how can you be so sure?"

"What if people stop supporting us? What if nobody comes to our fundraiser? We'll have to shut down the shelter for sure," Zara says.

"Maybe that's what they want."

"Who?"

"Just think. There are people who'd prefer we weren't here.

Eric nods. "Especially after the new bill proposal."

"What bill?" Zara asks.

"Didn't you hear?"

"No."

"Legislation that will prohibit the sale of animals from breeders in pet stores. Only animals from shelters could be sold," Eric explains.

"Brilliant! It'll put breeders out of business," Zara claps her hands.

Eric nods again. "We could pass the fliers and ask people to sign the petition to support the bill."

"Absolutely. The breeders are the ones contributing to the problem of homeless animals. We should print posters about the bill and the spay and neuter programs and plaster them around town."

"But those programs cost money too. And it's something we don't have," Barbara reminds us.

"Then we need to collect money for that as well," Penelope declares.

***

"We did that many times. We tried everything. It's hard to get people's attention these days. With all the social media, advertising, and stuff, whatever attention we manage to get, it's very short-lived."

"Yes, but now, after the fire, people should be more sympathetic."

"Not with the rumors. People are outraged by the accusations."

"Which are totally fake!" I say.

"But how are they supposed to know that?"

"I think that pet shop and breeders are behind this," I say.

"They wouldn't dare," Zara protests.

"I think you're right. Who else could it be?" Penelope says.

"But what should we do about the rumors?" Zara asks.

"Deny everything," I say. "It's a bunch of lies."

Penelope keeps typing on her laptop. "That's what I'm trying to do, but it's been hard to keep up. These hateful comments are impossible to stop. I blocked the worst offenders, but they keep coming back, saying the same lies over and over, just under different nicknames. It almost feels like someone is telling them to do that."

I look over her shoulder at her screen.

"And what's that link? What's 'Happy Pets Day'?" I ask.

She clicks on the link that's at the bottom of one of the comments.

"It looks like an event organized by the Best Pets Shop," she says. "Oh, for crying out loud!" she exclaims.

"What?" everybody turns their heads to her.

"Guess what. It's on the same day as our fundraiser!"

"What the hell!?" I almost fall off my seat as I read the announcement. "You're right! It looks like the pet shop teamed up with local breeders to do a competing event—on the same day!"

Barbara rubs her temples and asks, "When did they announce it?"

"A couple of hours ago."

"It can't be a coincidence," Barbara says out loud, what we're all thinking. Her phone buzzes, and she steps outside to take the call.

"You're right. It may not be a coincidence at all. Listen to this," Penelope says and starts reading. "It says here on their website: Come and see our puppies on sale at the weekend of fun for the whole family. All our dogs and cats are fed organic, humanely raised, pure meat. We love and take good care of our animals and take every measure to ensure their well-being."

"You think the breeders are behind this?"

"It's possible," Eric says.

"Of course they are," I say firmly.

Barbara, who's been talking on the phone with someone outside, walks back into the office and says, "Guess whom I just spoke to—Peter Johnson, the pet shop owner from our town. He told me about the 'Happy Pets Day' event, which according to him, they'd been planning for months. He said he was sorry about the fire and that he hoped that we recover soon. He also suggested that we join forces and do our events together. He went on and on about how much we had in common since we all had the best interest of animals at heart. He sounded like a nice guy."

"There's no way we'll be doing an event with them," I say.

"It may be our only option."

"Let's just change the date," I suggest. "We can reprint the fliers."

"It's too late; people will get confused. And what if nobody comes and we raise no money? That would be much worse than agreeing to that," Barbara argues. "He has one condition, though, that we don't support the legislation to reduce the breeding of dogs and cats."

"So, we should team up with the pet shop and breeders and don't support the bill?" Eric asks. "These laws have a chance to address the heart of the problem of too many animals."

"If we reject their offer and go it alone, we risk not raising enough money because of that backlash against us."

Penelope opens her eyes wide, staring at the screen. "Oh, no!" she growls.

"What?"

"They say the entire fire department will be their event. They're going to celebrate the firemen who saved the animals."

Everybody looks at me now.

"Didn't the firemen agree to work with us?" someone asks.

"They did." I nod.

"Is it possible that they changed their mind?"

"Olivia should talk to them again and see if anything has changed," Penelope says, turning to me. "After all, Ryan Kowalski is adopting Ruffy. And he likes you."

"No, he doesn't," I protest. "And what's that supposed to mean?"

Penelope shrugs. "Nothing. Just saying."

"They are on board, but we need to act fast," I say. "So, what's the plan?"

"Fortunately, in the digital age, everything can be done quickly. The photoshoot is on Friday, and we have a couple of days to set up the online store, print t-shirts, calendars, and other stuff for sale."

Did the firefighters agree to work with the pet store? I knew that asking Ryan was a bad idea, but nobody listens to me.

Penelope should do it, not me. I'm not good at sweet-talking guys into doing things. I just hope the whole thing won't turn into a massive disaster.

16.

RIGHT THEN, THE DOOR TO THE OFFICE flings open.

"I'm back," Ryan Kowalski says, with a grin on his face. He sure knows how to make an entrance. It's obvious he's used to attracting attention, acting as if we were sitting there, holding our breaths, expecting him, waiting for him to save us. Which we kind of were.

"I'd like to see Ruffy," he says. He must have noticed our grim faces because he adds, "If it's not a good time, I can come back later."

"No!" Barbara protests. "Olivia will take you there."

I look at Barbara with a why-me frown, which Barbara pretends not to notice. I take the keys and walk towards the door.

"Do you need help?" Eric asks.

"I'm good, thanks," I say. "Please, follow me." I motion to Ryan.

We step outside, and I point to the section where Ruffy's kennel is located. We walk briskly. It's beginning to rain, so Ryan hastens his pace, and I'm almost running, trying to keep up with him.

"I'm super pumped about adopting him," he says. "This is like fate or destiny that has brought us together."

I don't say anything, as we keep on walking. I wish I could adopt Ruffy, but there's no way he'd get along with my other dogs. He's so unruly; he'd need to be socialized first. And finding an apartment with four dogs would be mission impossible. With three, it was already hard enough. If I weren't so broke, I'd consider buying my own house.

As we get closer, something doesn't look right. Then I realize what it is. Ruffy's kennel door is slightly ajar. The lock to the kennel broke again, and Eric was supposed to fix it but probably forgot.

I run to see if Ruffy is there, but the kennel is empty.

"Oh, no!" I grab my cell phone and dial Penelope's number.

"Olivia, what's up?" she answers.

"Did somebody move Ruffy?" I ask. "He's not in his kennel."

"He was there in the morning."

"But now he's gone," I shout. "How is that possible?"

"Calm down, Olivia," Penelope says.

"I am calm!" I yell, not sounding calm at all. "We must find him! We need people searching for him!"

"You're right. But Barbara and Zara are gone for the day, and I must leave soon too," Penelope says.

"I can help," Ryan offers, but I ignore him.

I run to the office. "Ruffy is missing," I announce frantically.

"He should be in the kennel," Eric says. "That's where he was this morning."

"But he's not there now!" I shout. "When have you seen him last?"

"Last night, when I washed the kennel."

"Did you lock the door?"

"Of course, I did," Eric says, but I'm not sure I can trust him.

There was so much commotion during the last couple of days, with the fire and all the people coming in, wanting to help out, the shelter wasn't the most organized place.

"Are any other animals missing?"

"No. The two dogs and three cats that escaped when we opened the cages during the fire had been found and brought back to the shelter. We didn't even notice that Ruffy wasn't here."

"I'm going to check the neighborhood. Maybe he's in the park across the street."

"I'll go with you," Ryan insists.

"There's no need."

Ryan isn't the type of man who takes no for an answer. "If two people are looking, there's a better chance we'll find him," he argues.

I glance at him with gratitude.

"Let's not waste any more time," he says. "We can start around the shelter and then widen the search. He probably didn't get very far."

"I hope so," I say, looking into his annoyingly blue eyes that express deep concern.

I do hope Ryan Kowalski is right.

17.

Several other people volunteer to help, so we decide to split into teams to cover the area around the shelter.

"Let's go to check out the park by the river first," I say. "We often went there for a walk with Ruffy. There are some homes there, but it's mostly bushes and abandoned buildings."

"Okay." Ryan nods and zips up his jacket.

We walk outside. The rain is pouring down now. I'm glad I have a long raincoat and water-resistant boots. Walking in the trees, we keep calling Ruffy's name. Walking around in the rain in the park feels surreal. I remember the last time I was looking for a dog in the rain like that. It was just like I stepped back in time again. Except I'm not a little girl any longer, looking for my beloved puppy. And my life is a mess, just like my mother's.

But this time, I'm not looking alone. There are people here with me, helping me.

I glance at Ryan, trying to be discreet. Why is he even doing that? He didn't have to come. So, he wants to adopt a dog, but why this dog? Why does he want Ruffy so badly? Can't he just pick another animal?

I sneak a peek at him again, but this time he catches my glance, so I turn away quickly.

Ryan's phone beeps loudly, and he answers the call. I manage to see the caller's name. Anastasia. "Give me twenty minutes, and I'll be there," he says into his phone. Then he turns to me, "I must go now, but I'll come back later and help you look for Ruffy."

So much for searching together. Ryan must have noticed the disappointed look on my face. "We'll find him, don't worry," he says. I know he's just saying that to make me feel better, but he sounds so determined, I can't help but believe him. He dials a number on his

58

phone. "I'm going to notify the local animal services and police; maybe they'll see him in the neighborhood," he says.

We keep walking in silence. Water is dripping from the trees, and I feel my shoes filling up with cold liquid.

"I read an article by some guy, explaining how trees communicate with each other and how they react to different stimuli. How can you be sure they don't feel something that is similar to pain?" He points at the trees around us. "Don't you vegans care about plants? Where do you draw the line?"

Ugh. The plant-have-feelings argument. I must have heard it dozens of times, if not hundreds.

Then I look at him. He seems genuinely curious. There's no sign of his usual smirk on his face, or he's just masking it well.

"I don't know anything about plant communication," I admit. "What I do know is that plants don't scream or fight for their lives when you cut them. And that's good enough for me," I say. I stop and listen intently. "Did you hear that?"

"Trees crying?"

I ignore his attempt at humor. "I thought I heard a dog barking," I say. I listen again, but there's nothing, so I keep walking.

"Sure. One of the main arguments against veganism is that everybody should be free to make their own choices. We should all mind our own business and stop getting emotional about what other people have—or don't have—on their plates. As if it's a neutral lifestyle decision, like countless others that we make each day." I start panting as I walk faster and talk faster. "But choosing whether or not to consume animal flesh is not about personal freedom, or economic freedom, or any other freedom. Personal choice is when you choose where to spend your next vacation, but NOT when there is deliberate exploitation, suffering, and ultimately killing of living, breathing, and feeling beings." As I say it, I trip over a branch, and Ryan catches me before I fall into a muddy puddle.

"But aren't vegans a bit overdramatic?" he asks. "People have been eating meat since the beginning of time. Most people aren't going to change. So, why bother? One person saving a few animals can't possibly make any difference in the grand scale of things."

How can he even say that? I think with indignation, and then I remind myself that I used to think that too.

"People have been dying in fires for millennia. In fact, we're all going to die. So why bother?" I reply. "One fireman saving a couple of individuals can't possibly make any difference in the grand scale of things."

He nods. "Okay. Fair enough."

"I had been eating meat most of my life, too, and had been mostly oblivious to that hidden reality. I knew it was there, but I had no idea what to do about it. It seemed so overwhelming. I started reading books on the topic, and some of them made it more confusing, but I also found some that made it really clear. And one day, I understood that I couldn't participate in the exploitation any longer, and I went vegan. Just like that. On the spot." I stop, realizing I'm rambling, and he probably isn't even listening.

Ryan nods, which can mean understanding or basic politeness.

Suddenly, I hear barking again, this time much closer, and my heart starts pounding. "Did you hear that?" I grab Ryan's hand and squeeze it hard, and Ryan stops to listen.

I let go of his hand and run in the direction of the buildings surrounded by a tall fence. Now I can hear several dogs. I try to make out the different voices and think I recognize Ruffy among the others.

We come up to the fence and walk along it to find an entrance.

"How do we get in?" I ask.

"Hold on. I'm going to call someone," Ryan says and dials a number.

"What if they are in danger?" I say impatiently. I'm pretty sure I can hear Ruffy now. The rain keeps pouring down, and water in the river is getting so high, a part of the yard is beginning to flood.

"What if they need help?" I ask.

Thankfully, we find the entrance, which isn't locked, and we enter the yard.

"Ruffy!" I shout excitedly and point at a dog tied with a rope in the backyard of what looks like an abandoned house. "That's Ruffy! We must get him."

"We can't just break in and take animals off someone's property."

The dogs can hear us now and start barking even louder.

"If you're not comfortable doing that, then I'll do it."

"Okay, fine. I'll go. You stay here and watch if anybody is coming."

He enters the yard, and I follow him.

He unties the rope and carries the dog out safely, just like the night of the fire. The dog doesn't bark or try to bite him. I can hear dogs are barking inside the house and go inside. There are rows of cages with dogs and puppies. Some dogs are walking around freely; others are locked inside.

Some animals look famished; some of them are visibly ill.

"It looks like an illegal puppy mill," Ryan says as he walks in.

My heart stops. "Oh my!" I moan. "What are we going to do with all of you?"

"I've already notified the police. I know a detective who handles animal abuse cases," Ryan says.

"I don't think Ruffy is here," I say." Have you seen him?"

"No. But, hey, we'll find Ruffy, okay?" he says as I blink back my tears. Ryan's phone beeps again. "I'll be there in ten minutes," he says and turns to me. "I must go now; we have a fire alarm."

I walk back to the shelter, thinking about all the dogs and puppies we found and what will happen to them now. We can't take all of them in; there's just not enough space after the fire. We're at full capacity. The regulations don't allow us to take any more animals, so we'll have to send them to other counties.

Later that night, as I browse through some files on the shelter's computer, I learn that Ruffy came from that mill. Then he was sold to a guy who abused him. The owner denied the allegations, but there were witnesses, and eventually, the dog was taken away from him on cruelty charges.

Where is Ruffy now? Perhaps the previous owner steal him back?

And if so, where did he hide him?

18.

"Olivia, why don't you come to the city council's meeting today," Eric asks when I get to the shelter in the morning. "This is important. It's exactly the laws that we need in this town."

"What laws?" I ask distractedly.

Eric sits on my desk. "Remember the bill I told you about? The one about pet stores only allowed to sell animals from shelters, not from breeders?"

"Yeah," I nod.

"Over two hundred towns already have those kinds of bills," Eric says. "It's really important."

Penelope nods. "I read an article about cities voting to ban the sale of non-rescue dogs and cats in pet shops. The sale of puppies under eight weeks old will be banned."

"Sorry, but I don't have time," I say, evasively. "Barbara asked me to fill out these forms. This is important, too," I reply. I don't want to sit there for hours, listening to futile discussions over some seriously flawed law, when there's so much to do here—real, meaningful work.

"And what are these? Perhaps I could do that." Penelope glances over my shoulder.

"Insurance forms and applications for financial help. Why don't you go to the meeting?" I ask Penelope.

She tilts her head and looks at me from under her long eyelashes. "Maybe we'll both go," she proposes.

Why does she say that? She knows that I don't want to get involved in politics. I told her many times what I think of politicians (they're mostly corrupt liars) and politics (it's dirty). And laws only protect those who are in power.

"Isn't your father a politician, Olivia?" Zara asks.

62

I ignore the question.

"Does it say anything about the breeders?" I ask.

"Not really," Eric says.

"So it's another piece of legislation that's practically useless," I say. "Don't you see? The pet shops aren't the problem. The breeders and people who're buying from them are. And the irresponsible owners who neglect to spay and neuter their pets. This does zero to stop the puppy mills."

"You say this like it is a bad thing," Eric says.

"Because it is," I say. "This law changes nothing."

Penelope shakes her head. "It will potentially help find homes for hundreds, if not thousands, animals in shelters."

I roll my eyes. "Until we abolish the use of animals and the status of animals as property, nothing will change," I insist.

Penelope frowns. She stands in front of me, hands on hips, and asks: "Why, Olivia? Why?"

I look at her, blinking fast, not understanding.

"Why does it always have to be all or nothing for you, Olivia? Stop being so negative all the time. Yes, it may not be ideal, yes, it may not solve the problem, but it's a start. Passing laws like that goes a long way toward changing the minds of people and public officials."

Zara and Eric nod in agreement. They're so naïve.

Why can't they see the truth for once?

"At the very least, it will help people realize that there's a direct link between the industry and the millions of dogs and cats in shelters around the world euthanized each year because there aren't enough good homes for them," Eric says.

"That's what we should do here too. Pass legislation like that," Zara claps her hands.

"You know what? I think we should all go," Eric says.

I shake my head. "It's not enough. We should make all breeding illegal or at least controlled. That's what we must be working toward."

Penelope folds her arms on her chest and looks at me defiantly. "Then why don't you do something about it? Didn't you study to be a lawyer? If you'd gotten your degree, you could do something about it.

Or get involved in politics."

"I didn't know Olivia was a lawyer," Zara mutters.

"She quit a couple of months ago, didn't you?" Penelope explains.

All I can do is shrug at their ignorance. "Lawyers and politicians don't create or change laws. The laws follow the social norm, not the other way round," I gush. "And the majority of people don't want any change."

Penelope gives up on me. She walks to the coffee machine, pours herself a cup, and takes a big gulp.

"Oh, so you think doing nothing is going to help," Eric says.

"Surely, I'm not doing nothing," I say, frustration in my voice getting more and more apparent. "I'm here, aren't I?"

"Yes, but being angry and negative, you are not helping the situation," he says.

"I volunteer at the shelter. I help animals find the forever-homes. Oh, and I'm vegan. That's more than most people do," I say. "It's more than most of you do," I add.

Did I say it out loud? Judging by their expressions, it seems that I did, and I really shouldn't have.

"Oh, sure. You're so superior. Aren't you a Mother-freaking-Theresa?" Eric sneers.

"Did you know that Mother Theresa thought that the poor should just stay poor? That helping them out of their poverty was wrong?" he says. "And that's what you're doing. Working with the poor animals. But not doing anything to change their fate."

"You think that being vegan and walking dogs at the shelter mean anything in the big scheme of things? Don't you think you could be doing so much more?" Penelope asks.

I sigh heavily. What do they want from me?

"Okay, I'll go to the stupid meeting," I say. "But don't blame me if it just turns out to be a disappointment and a huge waste of time."

***

So the three of us go to the town hall and sit patiently, waiting for our turn for what seems like forever. And then, unexpectedly, the session gets adjourned, and discussion about the proposed legislation gets moved to the next meeting.

A couple of animal rights activists jump up from their seats and start shouting angry comments, claiming it's a setup and demanding a discussion and the vote.

I can't help but give the rest of our group a triumphant I-told-you so look. Eric squints at me and utters Arnold Schwarzenegger's line from the Terminator: "I'll be back."

19.

The next day Ryan comes to the shelter and asks, "Any news about Ruffy?"

I shake my head. "I was hoping you found him."

"No, but we're still looking," he replies. "I need to talk to you. It's about the photoshoot tomorrow. Some of the guys have questions."

"Let's go to the office then," I say.

"Actually, I thought about grabbing a bite to eat."

"I have work to do," I say, wondering why we can't talk here.

"Oh, come on. It's not like I'm asking you on a date," he chuckles, noticing my hesitation. "It's almost lunchtime. Even animal people have to eat."

I no. "Okay. But I get to pick the place."

"No problem. So, where shall we go?"

"It's my favorite Chinese place called Veggie Bamboo Garden."

"That sounds ... interesting," Ryan says cautiously.

"Don't make any judgments about this place until you've tried the food," I say.

He nods and winks at me. "Don't make judgments about people until you get to know them."

I roll my eyes and chuckle. "Fair enough. Shall we go now?"

Ryan smiles and follows me out the door.

When we pull up in front of the Bamboo Garden, I can tell Ryan isn't impressed. The place doesn't look like a five- or even three-star restaurant, by any stretch of the imagination; it's a non-descript building with a shabby exterior. Ryan raises his eyebrows but doesn't say anything. When I hop out of the Jeep and start walking up the steps to the front door, Ryan follows me.

Once inside, we see the place is packed. The tables are set close to each other and are all full of people. Chopsticks and forks clatter against plates and bowls, cups of tea clank against saucers, people are talking and laughing. A petite Chinese woman wearing a patterned silk shirt over black pants shows us to a table set for two in the corner of the room and hands us our menus.

When she leaves, Ryan leans toward me and says, "There are rumors that you've been serving dog meat to your dogs."

I shot him an appalled look. "Yeah, and there are rumors that some American restaurants have dead pigs and cows on their menu," I retort.

Ryan blinks. "I know. Those are ridiculous," he bursts out laughing.

"You know people do eat dogs in China," I say.

"Yes, but this is not China. And it's happening here, in our town. Didn't you hear?"

"I did."

"And you decided to pick a Chinese place?"

"Don't worry. This is entirely vegan."

He points to the menu, "It says here beef, chicken, pork."

"That's what they call it, but it's all plant-based. It's just to give people an idea of what it tastes like."

"And is it any good?"

"I think it is."

Ryan nods. "Okay, then, let's eat. How about you choose something for both of us," he says and puts his menu away.

I agree and motion to the waitress that we are ready. The waitress comes I ask her about today's specials. After I place our order, she takes the menus away and writes down something on her tablet.

About fifteen minutes later, Ryan announces, "Here comes our food." The waitress sets two plates of steaming rice with carrots, snow peas, broccoli, and pieces of chicken, covered with a thick brown sauce in front of Ryan and me, plus two cups of green tea.

"Are you sure this is vegan? It looks like chicken," Ryan asks.

"Just take a bite, and tell me what you think," I reply. He does as I say. The food is warm and delicious, the chicken is cooked to perfection, the vegetables are crisp, and the sauce is sweet yet spicy.

"It's delicious," Ryan admits. "Now, what is it, exactly?"

"It's a vegan variation of chicken in garlic sauce. The 'chicken' is made of plants, but is prepared to taste and feel like meat."

Ryan looks at me suspiciously and then at his food. "This chicken tastes so real."

"Yup." I nod. "Vegan food isn't that bad, is it?".

Ryan takes another bite of the plant chicken. "This is much better than I expected."

After we finish eating, I show Ryan the final designs, and he loves it. Then I ask, "So, why do you want to adopt Ruffy?"

"I love dogs. Dogs are so transparent and spontaneous. They couldn't hide what they think and how they feel even if they tried. When they're happy, they show it with their whole body—their tails, eyes, ears—give them away instantly. And they can't stay still—jumping and trying to lick you, pressing their body against yours. I just love that about dogs."

I take a big sip of cold water and nod. "Yeah, me too." For some reason, my cheeks start burning.

"So we have something in common," he says. After a moment of silence, he asks, "Why did you decide to work in a shelter?"

"Because I love animals," I reply.

Ryan raises his eyebrows. "That's what everybody says. It's the short version; I want the long one."

"This is it, really," I insist. I'm not telling him my life story about an insensitive father who took away my puppy.

He notices my hesitation and says, "I watched you in the shelter from a distance, playing with Ruffy."

I nod and smile, remembering the scene. "I was teaching him how to sit, giving him treats as rewards."

"Dogs listen to you. And Ruffy didn't seem like a monster."

"No, he's not a monster," I concede. "He's a cute little dog that wants love and attention, like all of the animals in the shelter."

Ryan takes my hand and asks, "Don't we all? I'm going to give it to him, I promise," he says, looking me deeply in the eyes. "You can trust me. I'll give him a good home."

I nod and glance around uneasily. How long does it take to prepare the check? I don't see our waitress, so I sit back. *Relax, Olivia. It's not like he'll bite you or seduce you,* the annoying voice in my head says.

"When I started volunteering in the shelter, I was so naïve. I thought if I can just convince enough people to adopt, it would solve the problem. I didn't realize it wasn't so simple."

"What do you mean?" Ryan asks.

"It's like with an iceberg: what you see is just a small portion sticking out of the water, with most of the ice under the surface, where it can't be seen."

"How do so many dogs and cats end up in the shelters, anyway? Where do all these animals come from? It turns out the pet owners are a huge part of the problem because they allow their dogs and cats to have puppies and kittens. This blows my mind because number one—we are responsible for the over-population, and number two—for not taking care of the animals. I mean, duh! But I'm boring you."

He shakes his head. "No, not at all."

"People don't think about those things. Every time we have a pet that we don't neuter, once they have a litter—assuming we don't dump them in a shelter, we need to find them homes. By spaying and neutering, we can reduce the number of homeless animals significantly." I pour myself more green tea and continue, "Some people think it's cruel if we don't allow our pets to have babies. But most puppies and kittens end up in shelters—so it's better not to bring them into the world in the first place." I take the last few sips of the tea and continue, "Every time there is a story on the news about a lone kitten trapped in sewage or a dog rescued from a fire, and millions of people hold their breath waiting for the rescue crew to arrive just in time to perform a miracle, saving the poor, unlucky soul from sure death. But thousands of animals suffer and die in shelters, and nobody cares. It's depressing..." I look at him and notice that he's been watching me intently in a way that makes me self-conscious. Oh, no. I feel I'm blushing.

I dissolve my ponytail and try to hide my cheeks behind my hair.

"I agree. Absolutely. No animals should have to be killed," he says. Does he really mean it?

"That procedure, you know, where they put animals to sleep?" I try to remember its name, but all I can think of is Anastasia.

"Euthanasia?"

"Right, it sounds better than killing. But why not just say it like it is? I guess when you use a different word, it seems less dramatic. It quiets your conscience a little. But it's the same thing. And do you know what some of the reasons for euthanasia are? Some may be valid, like when an animal has a terminal illness, but others are bullshit. For example, lack of home or caretaker? Seriously? So many people are lonely that every animal should find a loving home." I stop, realizing I'm rumbling and probably boring him to death.

Ryan clears his throat and says, "You seemed so kind and warm with those animals. The way you interacted with them—playful and calm at the same time—reminded me of someone—"

I hold my breath and wait.

"My older sister," he says, finally. "She was so good with animals."

I notice the past tense and wonder what happened to her. Before I have a chance to ask, he continues, "Anna loved animals. And animals loved her back as if knowing that they were safe with her, that she always wanted to protect them and help them. Whenever there was a wounded bird or squirrel, she'd be the one to find them and take care of them. The way she interacted with them was natural and at ease, completely effortless, and yet—it wasn't as easy as it seemed when I tried it," he chuckles. "Animals never listened to me or respected me the way they respected her. It was as if she knew their secret language." He pauses, and I sit still, waiting for him to continue. By his voice, I can tell this is not a story with a happy ending.

"Where's your sister now?" I finally ask.

"She died in a fire that burned our home to the ground. She was trying to save our dog and our younger brother—and I never forgave myself that I wasn't there. That's why I decided to become a firefighter. I wanted to save lives. Our dog died in the fire as well. That's why I didn't want a dog or any other pet. But then, after the fire in the shelter, it was as if something inside of me shifted. I realize I want that dog more than anything. It was as if saving him opened a part of my heart that had been closed off for too long."

I nod and take his hand. "Don't worry; we'll find him, and you'll take him home with you," I say. "He'll be lucky to have you."

20.

I can't stop thinking about the dogs Ryan and I found. "How can people be so cruel?" I say to Eric. "And where is Ruffy? I'm so worried something bad happened to him."

"We'll find him," he says, but I can tell he's worried too.

I feed my dogs and let them out into the yard. Then I turn on the television to distract myself. There's a story about a puppy that got stuck in the sewage, and an entire fire department is involved in getting him out. I try to see if I spot any familiar faces, but no. Ryan is not there, and neither is any of his buddies.

Instead, an entire TV crew seems to be there, with cameras filming the entire operation and reporters interviewing witnesses in primetime on national TV.

"I don't get it. How come we are captivated by stories of a single animal being rescued by heroic individuals, but the fate of animals in shelters doesn't impress us at all?"

Finally, the puppy is freed from the sewage, and the story ends in a close up of the puppy and the journalist, who congratulates and thanks the crew involved in the operation. And I'm like—wait a minute? Is that it?

Let's pat ourselves on our backs until we give ourselves a backache for doing the right thing. Not us personally, but someone did something, and that kitten had been saved—so all is well.

Except it's not.

If you've ever been to a shelter—any shelter–you know that it's not. Of course, most people never visit those places—maybe a zoo or an amusement park. Perhaps they aren't even aware that shelters exist and that there are so many animals in there.

"People are afraid to go there because they are scared they may actually feel something, strong emotions, like pain, anger, despair, helplessness, powerlessness—gosh, they may even cry," Eric says. "They're scared that once they look into their eyes, they won't be able to stop thinking about them, perhaps unable to sleep at night, haunted by the image."

"I wonder what will happen to that puppy," I say.

"I'm sure they'll find him a nice home, now that he's famous."

I nod. "He's lucky."

"How do you know it's a he?

"I don't. I just don't want to use 'it' because an animal is not 'it.'" I say. "I think that is part of the problem that we treat animals as things—objects that we can use in any way we please."

So, everyone has been captivated by that story—but nobody gives a hoot about the animals in those shelters. Shelters that are over-crowded; where hundreds of animals are euthanized every day.

One animal saved—big news.

Thousands of animals put to sleep—no news at all.

Where is the logic in that?

And are we ever going to find Ruffy?

21.

When I get home, I check my voicemail for messages. One is from Grandma. She wants to see me. It's been my routine to stop by on my way to the gym, but lately, I haven't been going as regularly as I should.

"You are just like him," she says, greeting me in the doorway.

"Who?"

"Your father."

I shrug.

"Yes, you remind me of him. He loves you, you know. He knows he hurt you, and he's sorry. You should talk to him. He wants to tell you something."

Too bad, I think. And too late.

But I just say, "I don't want to see him."

Grandma takes my hand and looks me in the eye. "It's his birthday today. Why don't you give him a call?"

I shake my head. "I don't want to. Please, stop asking me."

She sighs and walks to the kitchen. "Tea or coffee?" she asks.

"Tea, please."

"He's very sick now. And he's in a hospital."

I should say I'm sorry, but I don't feel anything.

"Just promise me you'll think about it, okay? And don't think for too long, or it may be too late."

I roll my eyes internally.

"He wanted me to give this to you." She hands me an envelope.

"What is it?" I ask.

"Use it any way you want. Pay off your student loan or as a down payment on a house."

I frown. So now he wants to buy my forgiveness? "I don't want his money!" I declare.

"He's your father; it's your money, too. Take it."

Does he think he can just pay me for what he did?

"Your father wants to make peace with you," Grandma says again.

"But I don't want to talk to him," I repeat.

She pours tea into two cups of her exquisite hand-painted china. I remember admiring it when I was little behind the glass door to the kitchen cupboard. Grandma would only let me use it on special occasions, under close supervision. She told me it was very precious to her and that I'd inherit it one day. Lately, I noticed she's been using it all the time. Did she decide that life was too short to buy green bananas and save the best china for special occasions?

"Go and talk to him. You are, after all, his daughter."

Funny, he remembered it now. Where was he when I needed him? I missed him so much after he left us. "And if I don't?"

"You may regret it later."

"Is he dying or something?" I blurt out.

Grandma sits very still for a moment. Then she clears her throat and continues, "He isn't dying. But he is very ill. Look, he's my son, and I'm not going to defend him. But he's sorry for the pain he caused you and wants to apologize—"

"And my mother," I correct her. "The pain he caused my mother and me."

"And your mother." Grandma nods. "He wants to leave you money… an inheritance—"

"So, he's trying to buy my forgiveness?"

"No, that's not what this is about." Grandma shakes her head. "He isn't trying to buy anything—"

"Money was always most important to him," I say. "More important than family. I don't want it. It's the root of all evil. Money, power, and dishonesty."

Grandma shakes her head. She gets up, opens the cupboard, and takes out a plate with cookies. "I made your favorite kind, oatmeal, nuts, and raisins." She sets the plate on the side table next to me. They smell so good. They remind me of my childhood when Grandma and I baked these cookies together.

Is she trying to bribe me? The bribery gene runs deep in this family;

Grandma knows I never say no to her cookies.

"Money is not evil; it's neither right nor wrong," she points out. "These are all vegan, of course. Help yourself."

I take one and bite into it. Umm, it's yummy, just as I remember.

"Money deprives people. It deprived my father. That's all he ever wanted—to be filthy rich," I mumble, my mouth full of delicious goodness.

"I don't believe money is evil. Power isn't evil. It's what you do with it that counts." Grandma pours more tea into both cups.

"Thank you," I say and take a sip. "Just look at all that he did. His legacy—he should be ashamed. This tea is delicious, by the way."

"It's your favorite kind," she says. "And he's very sorry for all the bad things that he'd done—"

"It's a little late for it now," I say a bit too harshly.

"It's never too late. And you could use money. Money makes things easier. They say it makes the world go round..."

I hesitate before reaching for another cookie. "There are many more important things in life," I say. Cookies or not, she won't buy my forgiveness so easily.

Grandma gets up from her armchair and sits next to me on the sofa. She strokes my hair gently, removing my bangs from my forehead. "I see so much of him in you."

I hate to have them to the side like that, and Grandma knows it, but I don't protest.

"He had ideals, too, when he was young. He wanted to change the world, but we were poor back then. When his father passed away, and I was left alone, times were rough. And his desire for money, to make it in this world, veered him off the right track. He met some dishonest people and followed bad advice." She nods her head sadly. "But that doesn't mean you should reject his offer."

"I don't want his dirty money," I insist.

"The money is not dirty," she says.

I scoff and ruffle my bangs again.

"Just think about it, okay? It would mean so much to him."

She takes the plate with cookies away and puts it on the side table.

"I can't force you to take that check. Nobody can or should do that, of course," she says. "So you don't want to be rich, I get that. But quitting your job like that? I worry about you."

"It's my life and nobody's business."

"Yes, I know. But is it really the best way to live it? The best way to use your talents?"

I turn my head toward the window to avoid Grandma's gaze. The truth is I've been asking myself this question a lot and still don't know the answer.

"Just to be devil's advocate," she continues, "What if you were rich, Olivia? A filthy rich woman. Because if money rules the world, wouldn't you want that kind of power?"

I pause and ponder the question.

She's asking me, what if I ruled the world?

Wow.

That's a far-fetched scenario.

But if I ruled the world, it would be a very different world indeed.

22.

SHOULD I GO TO SEE MY FATHER? As I'm driving home, I keep thinking about what Grandma told me about my father and the money.

She can be very persuasive.

What would I do with the money?

For one thing, I could donate it to the shelter.

The problem is those who could help solve the problems usually lack the resources to make a difference, and those who have it mostly don't care.

I reach into my handbag to get my phone and notice the envelope. Grandma put the check in my purse! I feel angry she tricked me like that and want to rip it to pieces, but something stops me.

There's this image that comes to mind when people think about an activist and an animal rights activist in particular. Namely, most people think of activists as angry and bitter individuals, who often use aggression, shocking imagery, and other controversial methods to call attention to the problems they're trying to solve.

Another stereotype that gets perpetuated is that of activists being poor. I watched a video by an activist who said, "I don't probably need to tell you that there's no money in veganism. Most vegan businesses are very much on the underground since there is no real cash in promoting veganism. Most of us who got into this got into this because we wanted to save animals, not to get rich."

"So, not everyone is interested in making money; I get it. But the problem is that being poor affects your level of ambition," Penelope says when I show it to her. She's very much into positive thinking, money affirmations, and other such nonsense.

But now I'm beginning to wonder if she's right.

Perhaps there's some truth to that.

If you always feel like there is never enough to go around, trying to pay your bills, it's tough to think in ginormous terms when it comes to solving the world's problems.

Not having health insurance and just limping along day by day—it's tough. And when facing an enormous problem, like billions of animals having their throats cut every year, that really can produce a great deal of unhappiness.

"If, as a result of your passion and activism, you've been living on the fringes, maybe it's time to recalibrate," she said.

"Are you saying I should go back to working in a law office?"

She shrugs. "I don't know. Every single one of us needs to be kicking ass for animals and making as great a change as possible. And it's tough to do that if you're still living hand to mouth." Then she says, "This whole question of the scarcity mentality that emerges when you decide to devote much of your life to activism is worth grappling with. You may genuinely care about your cause and believe you are doing your best but feel it's something to do on the side because you cannot afford to do it full time. This is unfortunate because you could be so much more effective if you had more money, time, and other means available at your disposal. We need to re-define activism and find ways how we can be doing what we believe in while making a decent living. How about we show everyone that it can be a life of abundance—both spiritual and material—and not a life of limitation, denial, scarcity, and resentment?"

Usually, I would roll my eyes at her, listening to such a tirade, but today, she's hitting a spot.

"Money is not evil," Penelope continues. "Just because big corporations are using money in dishonest ways and abusing animals in pursuit of money, it doesn't make it evil. Money is just a resource that we should learn to acquire and use to our advantage for the greater good." She continues, "Just imagine what impact you can make when you reach the six or seven-figure level. Not because you want a private jet or luxurious house or drive around in a fancy car, but because you want to make a bigger difference. Think of all the things you could do if you stopped playing small, had the resources to step up your game, without all the guilt or shame, but feeling happy and thankful for it instead."

I shake my head and cover my ears in denial, and yet what she's saying makes sense.

The attitude 'I'll be okay if I just make some money to pay my bills' isn't serving me or the causes I support.

It illustrates the approach toward money where there is that constant need to apologize because I don't want to be an exploitative individual or a selfish, narcissistic bitch.

23.

"What if you had a million dollars to spare, or ten million, or more?" Penelope asks provocatively.

I snort. "I'll never in my life come even close to that kind of cash."

"How do you know that? What about your father's inheritance?"

"I don't know how much it is, but I doubt it's anywhere near that. Besides, I told you I don't want it. I don't want to be like him. Always thinking about money, always wanting more."

"Okay, okay, whatever. Then just use your imagination a little," she insists. "What if people like you and me—activists, vegans, eco-warriors, you name it—ruled the world, being super-rich, and able to spend that money any way we please? Wouldn't it be a very different world—pretty soon?"

I shrug. "Maybe. Probably. But it's completely unlikely."

"What if we brainstormed ideas, not just ourselves, but put our heads together in mastermind groups and think-tanks to come up with best solutions and then used that money to implement and support the best ideas and solutions to create a better world. And—on a personal level—wouldn't you like to do what you truly love and believe in, as well as be making a difference while making money—so you can keep doing that for as long as you're alive?"

She pauses, waiting for my reaction. When she doesn't get any, she continues, "Just think of all the things you could do if you stopped playing small and dared yourself to play big because the world needs more people like you. Here is an exercise I did recently, inspired by this coach I follow online, to shift my limiting beliefs about money. Ready?"

I nod.

"Allow yourself to believe that you can be making $10K per month, $100K per month, or more. Now, let's brainstorm some ideas to see

80

what you could be doing if you had $10K or $100K to spare. If you had $10K or $100K or more per month to spare, what would you do?"

"Um. I don't know," I say. "It's completely out of my pay range."

"Think, Olivia. Just think. Use your imagination."

"Umm. I could donate it to the local animal shelters and sanctuaries—and make a real difference for the homeless and abused animals. Plus, I could donate money to other causes and organizations—contrary to popular belief, vegans do care about the homeless and the sick and hungry children, you know."

She smirks. "I know. Please continue."

"I could print a million brochures per year promoting veganism and dog adoption and pay students to hand them out at the local universities—I've read somewhere that this is the best demographic group to target, with the highest conversion rate. More than that, I could pay for TV commercials to bring up the topic of veganism, animal exploitation, and abuse so that people realize how deep and widespread it is."

"Okay, what else?"

"I could pay a talented screenwriter, director, and producer to make a blockbuster movie that would bring the message of veganism, justice, compassion, and caring about animals to millions of people, and how it relates to the environment and climate change."

"Yes, good. What about your own needs? Wouldn't you want to spend some of it on yourself?"

"I'd buy a house with a yard and adopt a bunch of animals from our shelter, and not worry about them when I go to work or travel because I could pay someone to help me take care of them."

"Keep going."

"I could sponsor campaigns that promote positive change in legislation because, at the end of the day, that's what we need."

"Aha! What else?"

"And let's not forget about the wildlife. I could buy huge parcels of land and establish them as protected areas for the animals that live there."

"I like that. That's an interesting idea," Penelope chimes in.

"I could start a vegan restaurant in our town or a whole chain—and hire the best chefs to make sure they become the go-to places for vegans and non-vegans alike. I could hire the best scientists and chefs to come up with delicious substitutes for meat and dairy and roll out these products globally. Plus, I could organize events, with music, entertainment, food, and whatever else—to get people excited about becoming vegan and adopting animals from animal shelters."

"Okay, you can stop now. I see you get the picture," Penelope laughs at my sudden outburst of enthusiasm.

Just thinking about some of these ideas makes my skin tingle.

"The fact is that money is a resource. Money is also power. And having it matters because it can help us make a more significant difference in the world—if we could just get past our limiting beliefs."

"The reality is that we do have to think about money to live in this modern world, and it detracts us from doing most of the things we want to be doing," I say. "The ideal situation would be to be able to make money while living my passion. Wouldn't it just be awesome and ultimately, the best use of my time, energy, and life?" I say and add, "But come on. Is it even possible? I mean, maybe it is—because I see other people doing it—but is it possible FOR ME?"

Penelope looks at me. "I don't know. Is it?"

I chew on my pencil. "So are you saying I should take my father's money? Or go back to law?"

She shrugs. "It's up to you. No one can tell you what to do."

24.

"I can't believe they're organizing an event in Washington Park on the same day as our fundraiser," Penelope exclaims.

"Say what?" Zara asks.

"I know, it's outrageous. They call themselves Friends of Animals. All the local pet shops and breeders that sell puppies will be there."

"So, what should we do?" Zara asks. "Should we change the date? Ignore them? Maybe do it together?"

"Join forces with these people? Never!" I protest. "Friends of Animals? That's what they call themselves? It's outrageous. They are the reason there's this homeless animal crisis all across the country and why the shelters are over-crowded and have to kill animals in the first place."

"You know what I think?" Penelope asks. "I think it's not a coincidence. I think they're doing it deliberately to sabotage our event. Don't you wonder why the owner demanded the money so suddenly and gave us such a short deadline? Usually, he was very accommodating."

"You think they had something to do with it?"

"It's possible."

"But why?"

"They want us out. Now, with the bill being presented to the city council, it'll hurt their profits as people won't buy from them anymore."

"But we had nothing to do with the bill," Zara says.

Eric starts reading an article from his phone. "Listen to this: 'Pet shops' greed fuels the commercial breeding industry that keeps female dogs and cats prisoners inside filthy wire cages. Their only purpose is to churn out litters of inbred puppies and kittens who are then taken away and sold. This ordinance will serve as a deterrent, preventing the sale o animals from cruel mass-producing breeders that churn out puppies and kittens as if they were an assembly line.'"

"No wonder they're mad," Barbara says.

"It looks like we've made some enemies," Eric says.

"So, now what? Maybe we should change the date?" Zara asks.

"No way. It's all set," Penelope protests. "The media announcements, the press, all the invitations that we sent out—changing the date now will only confuse people,"

"Do you think this will hurt us?" I ask.

Penelope shrugs. "Not necessarily."

Barbara puts down her phone. "Guess what? I just got invited to the good-morning show on the local television station," she says.

"That's good news, right?" I ask.

"I'll go with you," Penelope offers. "We can promote our event."

Barbara agrees. Penelope is outspoken and very photogenic, a perfect television material.

"Does anyone know what they're doing at their event?" I ask.

"Some local band, and a surprise celebrity. Plus, a lottery with substantial prizes. With all these sponsors, they can afford it," Penelope says and adds. "But we have the firefighters. They'll be a hit for sure."

"Let's hope the firefighters save the day," Zara sighs.

"Isn't it what they always do?" Eric winks.

We all nod in agreement, wishing that Penelope's secret weapon will be effective.

"But what do we do about all those nasty rumors?" Cathy, the new volunteer, asks.

"What rumors?" I ask.

"Didn't you hear? Some absurd accusations that we use meat from animals euthanized in our shelter to feed our dogs. You should see the angry comments on our website," Cathy explains.

"No!" Zara gasps.

"Yes!" Penelope nods. "It gets worse. Someone left a comment online that we are selling dogs for meat to Asian restaurants as a delicacy for the local version of the Youlin festival, or some other nonsense."

"How can anyone say that? This is outrageous," I fume.

"I wonder who's behind it," Barbara mutters.

"It's obvious if you ask me," Eric says. "The pet shop and a group of breeders. Including those that are suspect of running puppy mills."

"It's total bullshit!" I blurt out, fuming.

"All those so-called friends of animals always keep boasting how much they care about their animals, accusing us of being the kill shelter like we're the ones creating the problem, not trying to solve the mess they're creating."

"They want war? Then, let's go to war!" Penelope declares, and we all nod in agreement, although I bet no one has the faintest idea what the war with these people might look like and how we even find them.

"So, what are we going to do?" Zara mutters.

"Let's start with cleaning the kennels and taking out dogs for their walks," Barbara says. "Whatever problems we're having, they shouldn't affect the animals in our care."

25.

Dejected after hearing the news about the so-called Friends of Animals shenanigans, we leave the office to do our daily chores.

"Look at all this misery," Penelope says, pointing to the dogs rescued from the illegal puppy mill.

"Now we must make room for even more dogs, which in the current state of affairs is mission impossible," I sigh.

"Barbara is making calls to other shelters in our county and neighboring states, asking them to take as many dogs as they can," Eric says. "Hopefully, some of them will say yes."

When we enter the office, we see Barbara sitting at her desk, staring into space, as if daydreaming.

"We must cancel the fundraiser and get real; we'll never make enough money to save this place," she says when she sees us.

"You want to give up now? Why?" Penelope asks.

Barbara points to her phone. "I just spoke to our landlord," she says grimly. "He wants to sell the property, so whatever we manage to raise won't be enough. And unless we have money to buy it out, we'll have to move."

"Move where?" I ask. "We don't have a place to go."

"And that's our problem."

Patricia, Eric, and I look at each other in disbelief. After all these years of hard work and sacrifices, we'll have to close?

As people come back from their rounds and hear the news, the spirit in the office gets gloomy.

"So, after everything we've been through, the shelter is in danger of being shut down!" I growl in disbelief.

"How much do we need?" Penelope asks. "Maybe we can organize another event, bigger than this, get some other celebrities to help. Plus, online sales are likely to bring on more money still..."

Barbara shakes her head. "We need a lot more, almost two hundred thousand dollars."

We give out a collective sigh of resignation.

"Can they do that? Do you think they already have a buyer?" I ask.

"There's no way we can get this kind of money from potlucks and mug sales!" Eric scowls. "How much time did they give us?"

"Till the end of next month. Maybe I can negotiate to extend it a little, but not by a lot."

"It's obvious the breeders and owners of the pet shop are trying to eliminate the competition," Sebastian says. "Clearly, someone wants us out of here."

"I wouldn't rule that out. All that came completely out of the blue. We've been struggling for years, but they were always very accommodating."

"So, what changed?"

Barbara shrugs and spreads her arms in a gesture of helplessness.

Zara groans. "What are we going to do now?"

"We can find another location, maybe even better."

"A better location will cost more," Penelope says.

Barbara stays silent, staring blankly through the window at the rows of kennels; she seems tired. "We must close," she finally says.

Silence falls as we consider the possibility.

"No!" I shake my head. "We can't give up now."

Everyone looks at me. Suddenly I'm the one being the cheerleader.

Penelope slumps on the chair heavily. "We can't get that kind of money. It's an entirely different ballgame."

I get up and start pacing around the room. "What will happen to the animals? They depend on us," I growl. "Penelope is right. We'll organize another even bigger fundraiser. Besides," I pause to consider an idea that popped into my head. "I have money. Maybe not all of it, but a big chunk. It will buy us time," I say, thinking about my father's offer. It will be a perfect way to use it.

"I didn't know you were rich." Eric chuckles.

"My father gave me a small inheritance," I explain.

"What? Your dad passed away? I'm so sorry," Eric says.

"He didn't. It's complicated," I just say.

"Olivia, you shouldn't. That's too much." Barbara protests.

"No, really! Maybe the buyer will back up. For now, we'll be here for another two months, and that's plenty. We'll have lots of time to figure out what we to do."

26.

"I have a theory," Penelope says. She takes her phone and goes outside. Barbara and I are watching as she talks to someone, shaking her head and pulling at her long ponytail.

Finally, she returns and says. "The Zumba girl."

"The Zumba girl is your theory?" I snort.

Barbara looks confused. "Who is Zumba girl, and what does she have to do with us?"

"She's the daughter of the Happy Paws pet shop owner," Penelope explains.

"She's what?" I ask, surprised. "I had no idea."

Barbara frowns. "Okay. So? "

"So—the owner hates us. And I have reasons to believe that they are trying to buy us out."

Barbara and I look at each other.

"Do you think it was a coincidence that they organized a picnic for the animals on the same day that we picked for our fundraiser?"

"So, you think they did it on purpose?"

Penelope nods. "My sister joined the Fit & Strong gym, and she goes to the Zumba class."

"And she heard about it while jumping around in leotards?"

"She doesn't wear leotards. The whole group went to the juice bar after class, you know, the one across the street."

"I know," I say. "I used to go there with Christian."

"Isn't your sister in real estate?" Barbara interrupts.

"She is," Penelope says.

I gasp. "That explains it. They want to shut us down,"

"They sure don't love us here. If there's no shelter in the town, that would mean more business for the breeders and the shop."

"So, they are the ones trying to buy us out?"

"My sister confirms it."

"Especially with the proposed legislation, prohibiting the sale of animals—if it passes, it'll mean that you can only get a pet from a shelter. It'll make breeders' lives more difficult."

"They would surely love to get rid of us—it would make their life so much easier," I say.

"And let's face it, the vetting procedure is too strict. We must change it and become more accommodating," Penelope says.

I shake my head. "It's for the good of the animals. "

"But we're making it too hard. Rejecting people based on what? Lack of back yard or holding a day job? Nobody is perfect. And even a home that's not perfect is better than no home at all."

"I'm not going to release an animal to just anybody who walks in and says they want a pet. Some people are just unfit for adoption. And you know how hard it is for the animal to be returned to the kennel."

"I'm not saying to give them to anybody. Do a background check, talk to them. But if you set the bar too high, then who's going to meet such impossible criteria? Not everybody is willing to give everything up for the animals as you do."

I bite my lip. Is she right? I know people keep complaining. The number of returns is at a record low since I took over the adoption department, but so is the number of successful adoptions.

"You need to loosen up a little," I hear Ryan's voice in my head. "If you give people a chance, they just might surprise you."

***

As we sip our coffees at lunchtime, I can't stop thinking about what Penelope said. The conversation returns to the Zumba girl.

"So, what are you saying? I should be less rigid? More understanding? And maybe I should forgive Christian when he calls again, apologizing, trying to explain how that woman seduced him, and it wasn't his fault?"

"Did he really call you?"

"About a dozen times."

We keep chewing our salads in silence.

Then Zara says, "Maybe, the Zumba girl was going after Christian to get access to you?"

"Spying on the shelter? That's ridiculous," I say.

"If she's the daughter of the pet shop owner, was Christian feeding her the information that was helping them to hit us in the most vulnerable spots?"

"I wonder if he knew that, or she used him?" Zara ponders. "Poor Christian. Doesn't he have a brain of his own?"

"Or his brain is in his private parts below the waist?" Eric chuckles.

I never had a high opinion of Christian, but this? "I don't think he'd do anything to knowingly hurt the shelter," I say.

"All I'm saying is that he may be telling you the truth. She may have seduced and used him," Penelope says.

"Which just proves my point that most people use others for their own gain. Nobody can be trusted. It just so happens that in this case, a woman turned out to be the one using a guy.."

Penelope puts down her fork and takes a sip of water.

"That's not what I'm saying," she says slowly as if talking to a kindergartner. "You don't write people off just because they did something that you didn't like. You give them the benefit of the doubt. You also don't shut them off just because they want something. Having an agenda is not wrong. Everybody has one, including you."

"Oh, yeah? What's my agenda?" I ask, but Penelope doesn't bother to reply. And she doesn't have to, since I already know the answer.

27.

The next day, a loud ring of my phone wakes me up at dawn.

"Now what?" I growl, getting up from my bed.

It's Penelope. "You'll go with Barbara to the morning show."

"Weren't you supposed to do that?" I mumble, still only half-conscious.

Unfortunately, Penelope came down with nasty flu, and she asks me to go instead. I check the time; it's four-thirty in the morning. Getting up at this hour is pure torture. But what choice do I have?

Reluctantly, I agree.

I get there before six-thirty, and I'm so nervous, I'm not even sleepy anymore.

And then I notice Anastasia.

"Why is she here?" I whisper to Barbara, but she ignores my question. Or maybe she didn't hear me. And then I realize we'll be doing the interview together.

No way! I want to back out, but it's too late. Besides, we must promote our fundraiser and ask people for donations.

"Anastasia Wright is the daughter and co-owner of the Happy Paws pet shop," the host introduces her.

"You seem are unhappy about the animal people wanting to limit the breeding and selling of dogs and cats."

"We place our dogs and cats in good homes. We're responsible breeders and pet owners," Anastasia says. "We love our pets, and they love us. By passing this law, you'll be denying those animals the right to existence. They have the right to live, and people have the right to own them."

The host turns to us. I open my mouth, but before I have a chance to say something, the host says, "There've been rumors going around that you've been feeding your animals with dog meat? What is your response to these accusations? Have you been feeding your animals with dead pets?"

"We feed our animals commercial grade pet food as well as food cooked on the premises, with vegetables, grains, and meats," Barbara replies calmly.

"And you don't sell meat from dead animals?" Anastasia sneers.

Barbara looks at her, appalled. Even the host seems to be taken aback by her bluntness.

"We do our best to find them good homes," Barbara says. "Few people realize that we're trying to fix an impossible crisis. Irresponsible breeders are breeding more animals than people want, and we're getting more animals than we can accommodate."

"But what do you do with the animals that nobody wants?" the host asks.

"Sometimes, we send them to other shelters. If we didn't do that, we couldn't accept new animals that are brought to us."

"And are those shelters no-kill?" Anastasia asks.

"Some of them are." Barbara nods grimly.

"But others aren't!" Anastasia points her finger at us in an accusatory gesture. "So, you send those animals to a sure death!"

The host looks at her sternly, indicating that she isn't the one to be asking questions.

This isn't going well. People will think we're some cold-blooded monsters.

"Those accusations are outrageous," Barbara protests. "I repeat that we don't do it now and never did it in the past."

I turn to Anastasia. "If it weren't for people like you, we wouldn't have the problem of homeless animals in the first place. It's because of the breeders and irresponsible owners who keep breeding their animals because they're 'oh so cute' or because they want to offer them as a gift for Christmas, or whatever. That's why we're in this crisis. There's not enough space in the shelters and not enough people willing to adopt. And you keep breeding more animals, which only makes the situation worse."

Anastasia points her manicured finger at me. "You can't deny people the right to own pets. The benefits of owning a pet have been proven again and again. Pets can make a person feel better when they are down and low. Pets will be there when you need them to and will always stay by your side," she gushes with passion.

I roll my eyes. "They have the right not to be brought into this world as someone's property and to be under the absolute power of a human who doesn't have their best interest at heart."

She shakes her head and bates her long eyelashes. "But we do have their best interest at heart. Absolutely!" she squeals. "You think you're so noble, but not really. We breed animals and make sure they find great homes. You kill animals. So who is the real friend of animals?"

"Animals are not yours to do what you want, so just leave them alone," I snap. Then I turn to the camera and continue, "It's a sad, sad fact that animal shelters are forced to put animals down because they simply don't have the room or resources to look after them. An estimated 2.7 million animals are euthanized each year; that's 1.2 million dogs and 1.4 million cats. Our dream is to have all the kennels empty. So please, join us next week at our event, meet our animals, and adopt! Adopt, don't shop!" I almost yell into the camera.

At that point, the program goes to commercials, and we're dismissed. As I'm leaving the studio, I bump into Anastasia. Thankfully, Barbara pulls me by my sleeve, and we get out of there before I can do something that'll get me on the front pages of the local papers.

28.

Still fuming after the interview, I head straight to the shelter. I mop and clean the kennels, feed, and walk the animals, all the while, I'm playing out different scenarios in my head of what I might have said.

I should have punched her Barbie-doll face, but that wouldn't earn me the brownie points for bravery and the shelter—the good publicity we desperately needed.

I can imagine the outcry that would start.

The producers might like it, though. A girl fight on a sleepy morning show would wake the viewers better than coffee and send the ratings through the roof.

Then I remember that at lunchtime, I'm meeting with the firemen and discuss tomorrow's photoshoot.

Should I tell them the truth about our situation?

Maybe Barbara is right, and we should just give up.

"Are you hungry?" Shawn points to the food on the table.

I shake my head without even looking at the food.

"I want to thank you all for agreeing to help us out in this difficult time," I say. "We appreciate your willingness to participate in our fundraiser." I pause to clear my throat and blow my bangs out of my face, then continue, "However, our situation changed since I last spoke with Ryan, and the event that we'll be doing will be more about adoption than raising money,"

"No problem," Andrew says. "We are happy to help. It's an honor to support your cause. Whenever we can do, we're happy to be of assistance. Here, have a slice." He shoves a big pizza box in my face with what looks like double cheese, extra-large pie with pepperoni and sausage on top.

"No, thanks." I cringe.

"So, you don't need money?" Ryan asks. "I thought you desperately needed cash."

"Well..." I hesitate. "We just hope to find good homes for all of the animals. Because, unfortunately, we're going to have to close."

Ryan's blue eyes get as big as the pizza. How can anyone's eyes be so blue, I wonder.

I sigh. I don't want to spoil the mood today, but they deserve to know.

"Actually, we need a lot more than that. We just found out that someone is trying to buy us out. So we'll still do the event, but it will be mostly about adoption—to find as many good homes for them as possible.."

"What? Really?" Andrew mutters with his mouth full.

"Can we do anything else?" Ryan asks. "We'll organize another event. Do naked photos, if we have to." He winks at me, and some guys start laughing.

"I'm not doing naked photos. My girlfriend would kill me," Andrew protests.

"Who'd ever want to see you naked?" Shawn laughs, and everyone joins him.

I smile. "It's a family event, so naked photos wouldn't be appropriate. Probably." I add, trying not to blush. Imagining Ryan naked makes me feel all mushy inside, so I sit down.

"We can do another press conference, take it to the media again, do more fundraising," Ryan offers.

"Our management sees no way out of this situation. We even received threats," I say, remembering aggressive comments on our website.

"Who's threatening you?"

"I don't want to make any accusations," I back out. "The bottom line is we stepped on some toes. The bill we supported, the closing of the illegal puppy mills ... Anyway. There are shelters in nearby towns that will be taking our animals, and we'll be donating the money we raise to those of them who'd be willing to do that."

Ryan scratches his head and looks at me with disbelief. "So you're just going to give up?" he asks, looking me straight in the eye as if challenging me. "After everything you've been through? I thought you were a fighter."

"I'm not a fighter." I protest.

Why is he looking at me like that?

"Then use us. Use me. I'm serious." Ryan says.

The prospect of using Ryan sends all kinds of unsettling sensations through my body.

Why am I having such thoughts about this guy? I should be focusing on the animals and the shelter, not him.

"How about a hot dog? Don't be shy. Help yourself," Andrew smiles and wipes his face with a napkin. His fingers and lips are all greasy.

I stretch my lips in a forced smile. He's trying to be nice, so there's no reason to be hostile; I remind myself what Penelope told me.

I examine the food on the kitchen table. A pyramid of takeout boxes with pizza, chicken wings, ribs, and French fries, plus a few plastic containers of Coleslaw and spinach leaves drowning in French dressing. The smell is nauseating. I can't look at those without thinking of the animals that they came from. 'If they have wings, they want to fly; if they have legs, they want to run...' a line from my favorite podcast rings in my ears. Looking at the animal parts now turned into pieces makes me cringe. I can't NOT notice it. Why is it so hard for everybody else to see?

I can't help but notice Shawn's protruding belly. Just like my grandfather's, it's a heart attack waiting to happen. Grandpa had diabetes and heart disease and died of heart failure all too soon. He loved his pepperoni pizza, as well as ribs, pork chops, chicken wings, and fries—the works.

What makes this situation more ironic is these guys are in the profession of saving lives. They're helping people and animals, putting their lives on the line, and, just a couple of weeks ago, some of them did that to save the animals from a smoking shelter. Still, now, here they are, condoning violence on their plates, eating parts of animals who were just like those cats and dogs they rescued.

The irony of the situation is so evident to me, but not to them.

Even if I tried to explain, they'd probably laugh at me or brush me off.

"Are you sure you don't want anything?" one of the firefighters asks me again.

I realize I'm staring at his plate filled with what used to be bird's wings, only now, they've been reduced to a few greasy bones.

"No. I'm good," I reply and smile bleakly.

"She is vegan. She can't eat any of that," Ryan explains.

"Just for the record, I can eat that," I protest. "It's not about what I can or cannot eat. It's just that I don't want to eat that. I refuse to participate in violence," I gush. "And since you save lives every day, I figure, you'd understand."

There's a sudden silence in the room, and I realize again I said too much. Reminding myself why I'm there, I smile.

"SHUT UP, OLIVIA! *Don't antagonize these men. They're on our side,*" I hear Penelope's voice in my head. That's what she told me when I accused them that all they were after was free publicity and women's attention.

She's right. Those are great guys. Why am I always so judgmental?

29.

Thankfully, Andrew changes the subject. "Ryan, do you remember what I told you last month. About the competition?"

"The triathlon?" Ryan asks.

"I've heard they're raising the prize this year. Thanks to a new sponsor, they can give more money to the winning team."

"How much?" Ryan asks.

"Two hundred fifty thousand," Andrew says.

Ryan whistles between his teeth. "A quarter-million dollars?"

"Yep."

Ryan turns to me. "Would that be enough?"

I look at him incredulously. "That would be more than enough. But first, you'd have to win it, and I imagine there are plenty of people trying to get their hands on that kind of money. And second—why would you give it to us? You'd probably want to use it for something else."

Andrew nods. "She is right. We could use the money to upgrade our facilities and equipment. And our youth programs—we could finally get them going,"

I nod and start walking toward the door. "Okay, guys. Thank you again. I have to go now," I say.

"We could split the money. Besides, we could do those programs together, couldn't we?" Ryan keeps talking. "We could create programs where troubled youth interact with the animals. There have been studies that show benefits. Aren't there even programs like that running in other parts of our county?"

"We should look into that, for sure," Andrew nods.

"It'd be a win-win-win situation," Ryan keeps talking. "Everybody would benefit, isn't that right?" He turns around to face his buddies.

"Just think, you guys. The triathlon is a great idea. It would give us a chance to shape up."

Shawn shakes his head. "I don't know."

"We'd need to set up a training schedule," Ryan says. "How much time do we have?"

"Enough. The competition is in six months or so," Andrew says.

"That's too long—the shelter will be gone by then," I say.

"So, let's do the fundraiser first, and then negotiate the extension of the terms," Ryan insists.

Peter scratches his head. "I don't know. People have jobs, families, firefighter duties, and now this? Isn't that a bit too much?"

Andrew gives him a nudge on the ribs. "You don't have a family. And you could use some physical activity."

"I don't even know if my doctor would allow it. I've been having some issues with blood sugar and blood pressure," says Shawn.

"Man, then you really need to do it!" Ryan says. "You're not even thirty, and you have a health record of a middle-aged man."

"I can lose those love handles, that's for sure."

"I used to have a six-pack. But I haven't seen it for a long time. Except for the beer six-pack." Andrew laughs.

"With all the pizzas, hamburgers, and fries we're eating, it's no wonder."

"What do you want us to have? Spinach and broccoli?"

Everybody laughs. "I'd like to see how you lift those weights on food like that," Andrew says.

"I think we should do it, guys," Perter says. "And then we'll do the naked calendar," he chuckles.

"How many do we need to have in a team?" Ryan asks.

"At least eleven. Then December could be the group photo. Twelve would be even better," Peter says.

"Then let's count. By the show of hands, who is in?" Ryan says. "One, two, three, four," he starts counting as more and more guys are raising their hands, "five, six, seven… Come on, guys. We need three more!" he says, and a couple of hands go up. "Eight, nine."

"Where's Joseph? I'm going to call him. I'm sure he'd join."

"Are you crazy? His wife just had a baby. She won't let him

participate."

"What about Jason?"

"His dad had a stroke a week ago," Andrew says.

"I'll talk to him," Ryan says.

"Then we need just one more. I'm sure we can find someone. Let's register, and we can worry about the details later."

My head is spinning. Why is he doing that? He probably wants to get even more famous.

"I have to go," I say. "Thank you all again and goodbye."

"We're in, Olivia. We can do this; you'll see," Ryan says.

He can't just quit, can he? And it has to be about him all the time. I have to get out of this place. "Okay. I'll see you around," I say.

I'll see you around? Really?

It sounded like I wanted to see him. As if I was asking him to call me or something.

Was I?

The little voice keeps yapping in my head, saying—come on, admit it, you like him.

SHUT UP, THAT'S ENOUGH! I try to whip my feelings into submission. I've mastered that skill to perfection. I can't let the emotions control me because it never ends well.

What was all that about anyway? Surely, he didn't think that these guys could win a national triathlon. He's probably the only one in good shape; the rest are average at best. And average won't cut it. And even if they win, by some miracle, why would they give their prize to us?

I mustn't get my hopes up; it's a done deal. The shelter will be shut down. It's the way it always works.

And I am not even surprised.

30.

As I'm walking through the parking lot, I hear steps behind me.

It's Ryan. "Olivia, wait! Still no news about Ruffy?"

I shake my head. "I'm going to drive around the neighborhood to see if I can find him."

Ryan looks at me, and I can tell what he's thinking.

But I'm not giving up on Ruffy.

I know that's stupid and hopeless, but—" I begin.

"Not at all." He gets into my car and says, "I'll go with you."

"Okay," I say, surprised but also glad to have company. So, we spend an hour scouting the streets and parks, driving around, asking passers-by, but no one has seen him.

Dejected, tired, and hungry, we end up in a bar and talking and munching on celery sticks and fries, sipping non-alcoholic strawberry margaritas.

"How did you decide to become a firefighter?" I ask.

"It's a long story."

"I have time," I say, making myself comfortable in my chair.

He looks at me with his impossibly blue eyes, and I blush.

What are you doing? I scold myself.

He'll think I'm interested in him.

"Remember I told you about my sister Anna?" Ryan asks and clears his throat.

I freeze, waiting for him to continue. After a long while, he does. "I couldn't help her; I felt so powerless and angry. I never wanted to feel that way again," he says, takes the last sip of his beer, and continues. "Of course, becoming a firefighter doesn't make me immune to these feelings, but at least I can help people who are in trouble, and that's important to me, you know?"

I nod. "I'm so sorry about what happened. You must have been devastated."

He keeps staring at his empty glass. Then he continues, softly. "That day I saw you, playing with Ruffy; something about you reminded me of her. She was passionate and fun. But she was also strong and determined. And she loved animals so much."

The waitress takes away his empty glass.

"Would you care for another one?" she asks.

Ryan shakes his head. "No, thank you. How about you, Olivia?" he asks, pointing at my glass, which is almost empty.

I shake my head. "I'm good, thanks."

"How did you decide you wanted to help the animals?" he asks.

I don't like to talk about myself, but after his confession, I feel I owe him honesty.

"Well," I start. "For as long as I can remember, I always knew I wanted to change the world. Make a difference. Do something amazing," I say and feel another blush coming to my cheeks. I release my hair from the ponytail and try to hide behind it. "I know it sounds silly. In fact, most people think it's silly—"

"No, not at all. I don't. I understand completely," Ryan interrupts.

"I was on this pathway of being a good student and girl. My parents wanted me to become a lawyer or a teacher: someone successful, a noble member of society. I started studying Arts and then switched to Law, but within less than a week at University, it hit me: I'm not actually going to do this. At some point, I realized that the law is not here to *create* change. The law always protects the status quo and then follows."

Ryan nods. "It's an interesting observation."

"Yeah, people don't think about it, because it's so important to follow the laws of society, because if we don't—there would be chaos and anarchy, but in terms of evolving the society and civilization to a higher level, laws don't help. They impede the progress, don't promote it."

Ryan frowns as if contemplating my words. I pour myself more coffee and continue.

"It used to be lawful to keep slaves, for example, or use child labor.

Or that women couldn't vote. It takes a lot of time and hard work of many courageous people to overturn and change such laws," I continue. "It takes civil disobedience or a revolution to make major changes. Both of which require breaking the current laws. The other thing, though, which I remember thinking about doing a lot, was being a writer. But that's not very practical, right? Of course, when we're young, and we have these dreams, these desires, this calling, and this thing that says 'I just want to create.' But then you go on, find a job, doing something sensible and practical, that pays the bills." I pause.

That is something I don't have at the moment. I needed to find a job to pay my bills.

"People think that I'm extreme, but if being normal means doing things that I consider wrong, things that are cruel, and violent, and terrifying, then I don't want to be normal, you know. And if I'm not cut out for the normal life, then so be it. I'm going to do my life my way—somehow!" I smile.

I'm afraid to even look at him. He must be thinking I'm so weird. "People don't understand. They don't see through the layers and layers of lies and conditioning. I can't see it either, for most of my life. But here is the truth about the truth. Once you know the truth, it's impossible to un-know it, you know?" My sentences are getting convoluted. "Do you understand what I'm saying?" I ask. I'm afraid I'm not making any sense. "The same way that once you see something, you cannot un-see it. You don't just forget. It's become a part of you. So, it sometimes feels like a curse. Seeing this violence and suffering everywhere, while everybody else is going about their business as if everything is fine."

Ryan keeps staring through the window. "You know, I've never really thought about those things like that. I mean, what you're saying makes sense—especially the part about being unable to forget. Once you see the suffering, the pain, the violence—it stays with you. You can't pretend it isn't there."

As a firefighter, I'm sure he saw his share of horrific stuff.

"The ability to feel more, see more, understand more. It's a big responsibility," he continues. "It doesn't mean that you have to be miserable, though," he adds and gets up. A new song begins, and he motions me toward the dance floor.

I shake my head no and say that I'm a terrible dancer (which may not be entirely true), but he just waits for me, smiling. Finally, I get up.

I do love that song they are playing.

The dance floor is crowded. We squeeze in between the couples and start moving to the rhythm, our bodies pressing against each other, closer and closer with each step. Each time he touches me, it's like a bolt of electricity goes through my body. The world around me is spinning. I feel alive and for the first time in months—happy.

I catch his glance again. Is he feeling what I'm feeling?

It feels so good to let go. Let this energy out. It's better than any workout I've had in a long time. It's even better than sex. Especially since I don't have any in since I broke up with Christian five months ago, or was that six? Whatever. Nobody's counting.

Suddenly, I trip and almost fall. Ryan catches me just in time before I land on a waitress carrying a tray stacked with food and beer glasses.

My eyes meet his, and before I realize what's happening, he kisses me. I close my eyes and just give in to the tenderness of his lips. And then, as if realizing what's happening, I stop and say,

"It's getting late. I think I should be going now. We both need to get some sleep before tomorrow. It's going to be a long day."

31.

The day of the photo-shoot is sunny and warm with a cloudless blue sky. Just perfect. Twelve firefighters arrive at the shelter to pose for pictures with animals, laughing and joking among themselves.

"Are you sure you want to show that to everyone?" Andrew, who's Mister March, points to the big beer belly of his friend, Ricardo, Mister September. "It looks like you've been drinking too *mucha cerveza.*"

Ricardo chuckles and grabs Andrew's love handles, "Look who is talking. Where's your six-pack? Hidden under that belly?"

Shawn joins them. "This is going to be a total flop. Sorry, Olivia. But who'd want to buy a calendar with them?" he sneers jokingly.

"It's too late now. Maybe you can start preparing for next year."

"We need to start working out if we want to do this ever again. The guys are all excited to participate," Ryan explains.

"Let's go meet the animals," Eric says.

***

We try to keep everything organized, matching each firefighter with a dog or a cat, making sure everyone is happy.

"Wait till you see the photos. They're amazing!" Penelope exclaims when she comes back after about a couple of hours hours. She uploads the pictures onto her laptop.

"Fantastic!" Barbara says, browsing through the files.

Eric frowns. "So, no bare-chested photos?"

I give him a nudge in the ribs. "It's a family event."

"All animals cooperated and behaved well. There weren't any problems at all. Plus, a few guys asked about adoption," Penelope says.

I click on the page with products designed by Penelope.

"Wow, look at those t-shirts and mugs! They're so cute!" Eric exclaims. "You did a great job creating the layouts. And the slogan 'love is forever'. So sweet!" he gushes.

"Let's hope people will like them enough to buy them."

"Look, I set up an online store using one of the print-on-demand websites. Since we have no idea how many of the items we need, I figured it would be handy to have an option to direct people to order online in case they sell out before the fundraiser is over."

"Do you think we'll get invited us to Hollywood, like in that movie?" Zara asks, jokingly.

"Let's hope people like the calendars enough to buy them," I say. "It's only August. Who wants to buy a calendar in August?

"Maybe we could do another fundraiser at the end of the year," Zara suggests.

"If we're still around," I nod grimly.

"With bare-chested photos?" Eric asks.

I roll my eyes. "Sure, why not? By then, we'll have nothing to lose." Then I add, "But why do you want the naked pictures of those guys? Even if they have six-packs, no one can tell, as they remain hidden under layers of flab. And you should see what they eat; their diet is just horrible—greasy pizzas, BBQ ribs, chicken wings, fries. Since none of them know how to cook, all they do is order fast food. All those calories and animal fats contribute to their waistlines."

Penelope gives me a stern look. "Shut up, Olivia. You're doing that thing again. Just stop it."

"What thing?" I ask, confused, and surprised by her sudden attack.

"Being judgmental. And preachy. Not everyone can be perfect, you know. They may or have time to go to the gym or eat the perfect diet. Because, you know, they have other obligations, like saving people's lives. And with all the stress, who can blame them for not eating right. Who are you to criticize them? The perfect vegan? You should be ashamed," she gushes.

"These guys are all excited to help us, and it's all that matters. We should appreciate them, not criticize them," Barbara nods.

They're right. Absolutely. I should keep my mouth shut.

Now, all we need is to spread the word. Keep contacting the local papers and websites, putting up posters in libraries and on community bulletin boards, handing out fliers in front of the local shopping center.

By the end of the week, with only a few days before the event, it's what everybody is talking about: the Firefighters and Dogs Fundraiser and our calendar.

And I can't help but become excited as well.

32.

"WE SHOULD ONLY SERVE VEGAN FOOD during the event," I declare at the beginning of the meeting. "If we are taking animals seriously, then we should take ALL the animals seriously."

We're discussing the details of the fundraiser so that everybody knows what they're doing, and there are no surprises; the discussion veers toward food.

Barbara massages her temples in a 'there she goes again' gesture. "How many times do I have to explain to you that we can't do that. People won't be as generous when there's nothing for them to eat," she says. Even though she's a caring and loving person, somehow, she can't fathom the fact that pigs and chickens suffer just like dogs and cats.

Why is it so hard to understand? I wonder, feeling frustrated.

Meanwhile, I'm still thinking about what Penelope told me the other day. Everything I said was true. But this time, even I understand I may have crossed the line.

People accuse me of putting me ideology above the good of the animals all the time, so I'm used to it. And the children. Chickens and pigs are more important to me than dogs and children. I wonder if anybody says that to Eric. I bet no one tells that to a gay guy.

I must prepare something special this time. But what?

"Nobody likes to go hungry. And you can't expect firefighters to be satisfied with rabbit food. How many times are we going to have this discussion?" Zara chimes in.

"As many as necessary to finally convince you," I reply. "It's really hypocritical of you to try to save some animals while serving dead bodies of others. Vegan food can be delicious. No one will go hungry, I promise." I make that point before every event and every time I'm outvoted. Most of the shelter employees and volunteers aren't vegan and worry that vegan food won't put people in a generous mood.

"You promised we'd do it the next time we organize a fundraiser," Eric says to Barbara. He, too, is vegan, plus Penelope is mostly vegetarian, but the rest of the crowd isn't 'ready' to give up eating animal flesh.

Barbara shakes her head. "The shelter is in trouble, we have no money to keep up its operations, and you worry about serving meat at the fundraiser? Stop putting your agenda before the interest of the shelter; there's too much at stake."

So, this time again, Eric and I are outvoted.

"But that doesn't mean that you can't bring some salads and other side dishes. You know you're welcome to do it," Barbara adds. "Just don't go overboard, like the last time. We don't have to waste food that nobody wants."

After several disasters in that department, I have to make sure my food is not only delicious but also attractive. The presentation is key when it comes to events like that. I don't want the food to look like a sad blob of green mush, especially since the food will be sitting out there for a couple of hours. I also have to make sure sauces and marinades are full of flavor, and there is enough salt and pepper. I don't want anybody to accuse me that vegan food is bland or boring.

How anyone can even think that is beyond me.

I decide to do some research. I've been reading recipes for barbecues and potluck, trying to choose recipes that would be easy to prepare and suitable for such an occasion, but still can't make up my mind.

I think about ordering from the Bamboo Garden but then change my mind and decide to go for something different. Instead of Asian, it'll be Eastern European. I'll order pierogi, hunter's stew, vegan sausage, and side salads from a place called White Eagle in Greenpoint.

"There's this awesome place I know with pierogi, freshly made and delicious," I say. "My friend has just become the new owner, and she'll give us a great price. I'll call her and check if she can deliver the food the morning of the fundraiser."

Everybody nods in agreement.

"Okay, fine," Barbara says. "I love pierogi. Pierogi it is."

33.

"I'm exhausted," I say, slumping on the sofa. After the whole day of working hard in the shelter, all I want is to go to bed.

"What are you up to?" I ask Penelope.

She's sitting cross-legged on the floor, headphones on, tapping herself on her face and head. "Even though I'm anxious about my performance review, I deeply and completely accept myself. Even though I'm worried about how to approach my boss, I deeply and completely accept myself. Even though—" she pauses as she notices I'm staring at her. "You're back," she says and takes her headphones off.

"What are you doing?" I repeat my question.

"I'm tapping," she says as if that explains anything. She must have noticed my puzzled look because she continues, "I'm nervous about my interview tomorrow, and this really helps me release negative emotions and overcome limiting beliefs. I'm almost done. I just need to do another round."

Not again! I roll my eyes. Affirmations plastered around the house, meditations, yoga, NLP, and now this. "Penelope, why do you need to do all this stuff? You're like the most positive-freaking person I know. What's there to release?" I ask.

Penelope takes a deep breath and slowly exhales. Then she rolls her head around in a circle and massages her neck with her beautifully manicured fingers. How does she do that? I can never understand how women could perform any menial tasks and still keep their nails immaculately manicured. Mine are always in various stages of disarray, from being broken and chewed up to make even (for lack of the nail clippers). Does she go to Tipsy Tips too?

"You'd be surprised. I have all these blocks of energy stored in my body. Someone recommended that I try this technique—and I love it!

111

You should try it too. I bet it would do wonders to your attitude," she says.

"Thanks, but no. My attitude is just fine," I grouch.

Penelope tilts her head and looks at me. "Really?" she says, and it isn't even a question. She puts her headphones away and gets up. "Do you want some water?" I shake my head no.

"I do," she says. "I need lots of water. I think all this releasing makes me super thirsty. And famished." She picks a banana from the fruit bowl, peels it, and takes a bite. "Tapping uses the body's energy meridian points by stimulating them with your fingertips. You're literally tapping into your body's energy and healing power. It's called EFT, Emotional Freedom Technique. It combines ancient Chinese acupressure and modern psychology," she mumbles, finishing her banana. She notices a skeptical look on my face. "Your body is more powerful than you can imagine. It's full of life energy and an astounding ability for self-healing. With EFT you can take control of that power."

I look at her, confused. "How do you even find all this stuff? This tapping-yeti-something—"

"E.F.T., Emotional Freedom—."

"Whatever," I interrupt her, "how is it supposed to help you with your review and talking to your boss? Punching yourself on your head and face—it looks ridiculous. Maybe you should just punch him."

"It's not punching; it's tapping. And it can be used for anything, from pain relief, to healing childhood traumas, to clearing limiting beliefs, to weight loss, body image, and food cravings, even fears and phobias. It's amazing! You just identify the problem you want to focus on and tap away. It could help you clear up some of your …,"—she pauses searching for the right word) issues,"—she finds it.

"What issues? I don't have any issues to clear."

Penelope stops what she's doing and glares at me intently. "Olivia, I've known you for ages. But you've changed," she says with concern in her voice. "You used to be different."

"It's called growing up."

Penelope shakes her head. "Not like that, Olivia. Not like that."

"And how is—THAT? What does THAT mean?"

"It means you can't keep isolating yourself from people and life.

You are young and attractive but act like an old person. You're like my grandma Mildred. Except she lived through the depression and grandpa Henry drinking himself to death. Nothing like that happened to you. You should at least try to be more positive. Lighten up a little."

"Huh? So I'm not positive enough for you? Not cheerful enough?"

"You are hiding behind the animals to shield yourself from people and relationships. You keep saying that animals are easy. They won't lie, cheat, or laugh about you behind your back. But they also won't challenge you, and they won't tell you the truth."

"Oh, so what's the truth?"

"The truth is your life is passing you by. You could be doing so much more, having relationships, and making a bigger difference. So you had bad things happen to you when you were little, but you're not the only one. It's not just you. Many people had much worse things happen to them, but they turned out okay. They move on. It's time to put it behind you and move on too."

"Easy for you to say..."

Penelope stands in front of me, hands-on-hips as if challenging me. "So your father cheated on your mother, and he gave away your dog. Is that the reason not to hate all men and not trust them?"

"So it's my fault that my relationships aren't working? That Christian cheated on me—that was my fault too?"

"I don't know. Was it? Maybe you're not giving yourself a chance to have a real relationship. You never let anybody close to you, Olivia. You keep them at a distance. You want to protect yourself from getting hurt, but that's exactly what happens because you never give yourself a chance for love."

I look at her, hurt. How could she say this to me?

"It's not just about the past. Those bad things—they are everywhere. I can't live pretending like everything is fine. The suffering of animals—it's everywhere," I say, my voice trembling.

"Ever since you became vegan, it's like you've been carrying the weight of the whole world on your shoulders. I mean, look at you! You're miserable. You're angry. You avoid people. You don't even go out with us for a happy hour anymore."

Okay, so that one is true. I used to go out with a bunch of our mutual friends on Friday nights to get some drinks and snacks, but lately, I'd been mostly avoiding that. But I had my reasons.

"That's because I don't want to watch people eat mutilated animal parts, such as ribs and wings. Are you saying that I need to change? Because if you do, it's not going to happen," I say.

"I'm not saying that. It's just the way you're acting—you are not making it easy for people to like you or want to hear you out. You make veganism sound so... painful. And complicated."

"What should I become some kind of Pollyanna, in a flowery dress, dancing and twirling on an open meadow, la-di, la-di-la, life is beautiful, let's all love each other and be happy? Is that what you want me to do?"

Penelope stands there for a moment, her body starting to tremble. She finally bursts out laughing. "No. You don't have to do it like that," she giggles. "You'd look ridiculous in a fluffy dress, twirling, and you'd probably fall over," she says, and I can't help but smile. She's right. I'm kind of clumsy.

"Be the change you want to see in the world—I hear you say those words on several occasions. That's what you want to be, right? The change. But look at you. Is that really the world you want? Where's the trust? Where's the love? Where is the joy? It's pathetic. Who'd want that? Not trusting one another? Not having real relationships? Not loving?"

"But going around like some Pollyanna, happy go lucky, chanting, tapping, reciting positive mantras, minding my charkas, and believing that my thoughts will materialize if I just keep believing in them? All that be positive and be happy approach at life; it's just making me want to throw up. Life is not like that. Just wanting to be happy is so ... I don't know... Shallow. Insignificant. And selfish."

"What's wrong with being happy? Or being normal?"

"If that is what it means to be normal, then I don't want it."

***

After the EFT session, we go into the living room, and Penelope pours us two glasses of red wine.

"Seriously, Olivia. You've been so angry, so resentful of people, so morally superior—how can anybody be attracted to that? How would anybody want to be THAT? You are not doing animals a favor because if that's what an animal lover and defender looks like—then you're not convincing anyone to change. No one wants to be miserable, wallow in negative emotions and pain," she argues.

I keep staring at my glass, admiring the deep color of the wine.

"Here's a newsflash for you—people want to be happy," she continues. "I really admire that about you, Olivia. Your sacrifice so much for those animals. But where are you in all that? You cannot neglect yourself and your emotions. To be able to help the animals, you need to take care of yourself first. You know, like on the airplane, they tell you to put on your oxygen mask first, then help the others. You need to put on your oxygen mask, Olivia."

As much as I resent her criticizing me like that, what she says hits a nerve. What if she is right? Then I shake my head. "This is nonsense."

"Oh, really?" Penelope growls. "You want the world to be filled with love and positivity and kindness—be that. And then see what happens. You feel like you fail all the time, but maybe you set your expectations wrong. You expect people to change instantly—and with that, you will fail every time. What if your goal was to saw seeds?"

"But I'm not a farmer," I grouch, trying to make a joke.

"You know what I mean. Sowing seeds by speaking your truth, without anger or judgment, without expectation of converting anyone. If that's your goal, then you'll succeed every time."

"This 'manifesting your reality' is nonsense. You say, believe, and it will happen—what a bunch of crap. If it were so easy, everybody who watched 'the Secret' would be a millionaire living in a mansion on a tropical beach. Here is a newsflash for you: there aren't enough mansions and beaches for the eight billion people who inhabit this planet."

Penelope raises her eyebrows and crosses her hands on her chest.

"Okay," she says. "You can dismiss the idea all you want, but that's exactly my point. It's not enough to just say it that you want it; there's much more to it than that. It works—but only if you give it your all.

Have you been giving your life your all?"

I keep petting Noah's and Zulu's backs, Penelope's two rabbits.

"Leave your closet, or your cave, wherever you're hiding. Let your light shine, spread your wings, and then see what happens. Then, see not just your reality change, but the world around you will be transformed."

As much as I hate listening to the new-agey mumbo-jumbo from Penelope about the "Secret" and manifestations, affirmations, and EFT, I have to admit that I've been angry.

Maybe even depressed.

But how could I NOT be?

Seeing how much wrong is in the world, realizing that it's not just my family, but the whole world is broken—it's more than I (or anyone) can handle.

When I joined an animal rights organization for the first time, we went for a clandestine tour of an industrial farm. The leader of the group knew someone at the farm, and we pretended we were students writing a paper on agriculture production methods. (Tthey would never let us in if they knew who we were.) We couldn't stay there long, but it was enough. I saw everything—the cages, the mutilation, the slaughterhouse. There was a young girl there with us who couldn't stop crying. But I didn't cry. I was just angry.

Looking into the eyes of those animals, I couldn't stop wondering what the difference was between them and the dogs and cats.

And I knew there was none.

All that I could think was: they are just like dogs.

They are just like us.

How could I ever explain it to someone?

And what happens when you explain it to someone, and you show them the pictures and videos, and they still ignore the truth.

"Olivia, you have to accept how powerful you are. For good and for bad—you are creating your reality with your everyday thoughts. With every action, you create a reaction, and every reaction is part of a chain reaction. With every thought, every motion, and every heartbeat, you are creating."

"Okay. If you say so."

"So the question is—what are you creating? You need to stop those negative thoughts, angry emotions, feelings of resentment, and limiting beliefs. Dissolve them and transform them into confidence, certainty, and belief. Realize that you have power. The power that comes from mastering your emotions and your mind."

She gets up, ready to leave. "You want to start making a difference? Then stop hiding and pouting and start being a kick-ass leader, like you are meant to be."

34.

My phone beeps, and I check my messages.

"The world needs YOU, Olivia." I read the title of the email all in capital letters. OMG. Did Penelope sign me up for one of her 'life-changing' newsletters? She swore it practically changed her life, and it was about to change mine, of course.

But this stuff is not for me. It's one thing to plaster the affirmations and positive quotations all over the house, a habit I found to be mildly annoying, but spamming my mailbox with those kinds of messages was just crazy.

Okay, I love Penelope, she's my best friend, but this? She doesn't expect me to follow this silly tactic, reading the Secret, putting positive affirmations on my bathroom mirror, fridge, and the wall opposite the shoe bench (so I would see them every time I went to the bathroom, to the kitchen, or outside.)

I knew that was just a tactic, using the person's name to personalize the title, to make it feel personal, like we are on the first name basis with the sender, even though I've never met her before), to entice me open the email, but still. It hits a nerve. I open the message and start reading.

"The world needs YOU, Olivia," I read out loud. "Right." I roll my eyes. "If it needs me, how come I never feel it."

No one would even notice or care if I disappeared from this world tomorrow. Then I thought about Charlie, Oscar, and Coco. Well, maybe they would miss me, but that's about it.

"You have ideas that the world needs to hear about.

You know things that others are ignorant about.

You notice things that others are unaware of.

You care about things that others think are unimportant, or simply they're too lazy or too busy or too whatever to take the time to explore.

118

You see things the way no one else sees them—understanding things the way only you can understand them, feeling them the way only you can, with your unique combination of strengths and weaknesses.

The WORLD NEEDS YOU TODAY because...

YOU are uniquely qualified to CHANGE THE WORLD by SPEAKING what's on your mind, by SHARING your message, and—most of all—by BEING ALL YOU CAN BE.

Unapologetically.

Fearlessly.

YOU."

I pause and shift uneasily in my chair.

"With all your talents, skills, and gifts.

With all your feelings, emotions, and quirks.

With all your struggles, weaknesses, and failings.

No one else can do it but YOU.

But and mind you, this is a big BUT....HUGE BUT...

... being YOU to your full potential takes work.

It's not automatic. It's not a given.

BECOMING YOU TAKES TIME AND EFFORT.

Warning: What you are today may not be the true you. Most likely—it's not. It may be difficult to tell which part is the 'true' you and which is other people, your family, the society, conformity to what's expected, the so-called traditions—that's why becoming the true you is not a given; it's not automatic. You don't become TRUE YOU just by being born and living your life.

You become TRUE YOU by digging deep into your soul, peeling off the layers, and discovering what's hiding inside of you—the authentic you.

You become TRUE YOU by finding your truth and sharing it with the world.

You need to PRACTICE BEING YOU every day.

You need to work at being authentically YOU every moment of your life.

Unapologetically.

Fearlessly.

YOU.

"I know it sounds strange. It's confusing—how come I need to WORK at something that should be automatic, spontaneous, and natural—that doesn't make any sense, right?

I nod.

"And yet, when you think about it, it does. It makes perfect sense. If you don't work at being YOU, you become other people. You conform to what society expects from you.   You become what your parents always wanted for you. You inhale their fears, their wants, beliefs, and aspirations—and you get confused by accepting what's not fully yours.

Sometimes it's difficult to see where other people end and you begin. We like to talk about being independent and free—but we don't want to stand out too much.

So in the process, we become an AVERAGE of what is out there.

The AVERAGE—which means you're condemning yourself to mediocrity. To being normal—whatever that means. Being ordinary, instead of extraordinary. Being like everybody else. Not a bad thing, but not a great one either.

So it may take a lot of WORK to become a real you again.

Most people won't do it. They're too busy doing other things, too lazy doing nothing in particular or simply cannot be bothered.

But you—you are different.

You are not most people.

So let me ask you this—

Are you at least curious about what's hiding inside? What are you capable of? Do you have a feeling that there's more—more to DO, to EXPERIENCE, to FEEL?

Are you ready to be re-born?

Are you ready to unleash the power of YOU into the world?

If not now, then when?

If not you, then who?

Let's change the world TOGETHER, SOONER, rather than later."

Dogs started barking joyfully, greeting Penelope, who brought them delicious snacks.

"Stop spoiling them!" I shout.

Am I becoming a grumpy old maid?

I close my laptop and jump out of bed.

I decide to start the day right by making a pitcher of deliciously green smoothie. As the preparations for the fundraiser are gaining speed, we have a lot of work ahead of us.

35.

Whenever I need to work off some extra energy, I take my dogs for a long walk. But sometimes that's not enough. On such occasions, I head to the local gym.

After the fiasco with Christian, I wanted to find another fitness club, but they refused to cancel my membership. I walk into the ladies' changing room and quickly put on my workout outfit. When I finally leave the locker, I'm surprised to see so many people. Usually, it's much quieter at this hour, before the after-work crowd starts to arrive. This time, I see a group of hunky men hanging around the free weights area.

The men look familiar. I try not to stare, but the young woman in tight spandex isn't shy about it, as she whispers excitedly into the ear of her friend. Now the two of them look at the group with puppy eyes.

I decide to move to a different gym section, just as the door to the fitness room swings open.

I'll be damned! Like I needed to see her again!

The Zumba Girl. Anastasia-freaking-Steele.

Or whatever her name is.

I didn't think I'd see her here since she works for the competition.

What is she doing here, anyway? Fortunately, she doesn't notice me. I don't need another argument or a fight right now.

"Yoga will be starting in just five minutes," she announces.

The men start walking into the big classroom, grabbing mats, and spreading them on the floor.

"So now the Zumba girl is branching into yoga?" I whistle under my breath as I hear the familiar voice say my name, "Are you joining the yoga class, Olivia? The instructor is really good."

I look up and only see his back, but then he turns around.

It's Ryan! He looks different in spandex. I hardly recognize him without his usual gear.

I shake my head and watch incredulously as the firefighters from Engine 13, lead by Ryan Kowalski, walk into the room and start spreading their mats.

So they're going to flex into pretzels and meditate? They don't look like the type to me. I'd imagine they'd be more into weight training, boxing, or martial arts, not yoga.

I can't hear what they talk about, but I can see Anastasia's wide smile. Ryan Kowalski comes up to her and starts introducing his buddies.

Barefoot and tanned, she looks gorgeous. Long, blond hair, fashionable gym clothes tightly fitting her shapely body.

Should I warn Christian not to put too much emotional investment into this relationship?

Nah. What do I care?

I feel a tingling sensation in my stomach. Does Ryan like her too?

Stop it, Olivia. You're imagining things.

I grab the heaviest dumbbell I can lift and start doing arm presses, not caring about the form, just wanting to unload the emotions, until my muscles begin to burn and then go limp, refusing to do any more heavy lifting. I drop to the floor, exhausted, and glance at the clock on the wall. I should be heading home.

In the shower, all sore and tired, I decide to wait for Ryan and ask him about any news about Ruffy. But when he finally appears, a tall blond girl waving excitedly at him from the parking lot.

She comes up to him, and he puts his arm around her neck in a gesture that seems both relaxed and comfortable like they're in a long term relationship. The guy is popular. They look like a great couple.

Oh, boy, do I feel silly.

How could I be so naïve?

36.

Over the next few days, I keep avoiding Ryan, sending his calls to voice mail, and not answering his texts.

Two days later, as I'm wandering around the parking lot of the local farmer's market, searching for my car, I hear the familiar voice calling my name.

"Olivia, wait! Can you tell me what's going on? I left you several messages. Don't you think you owe me an explanation?"

I don't owe you anything, I want to say, but do my best to remain calm. "I've been busy. Besides, this isn't going to work."

"What's not going to work?"

"You know..." I say.

He seems taken aback. "We haven't even tried."

"We're just... too different," I say.

He shrugs. "And how's that a bad thing? Everybody is different. Different is good."

"There are certain things that are very important to me; I just can't be with someone who doesn't share the same view of the world."

"I don't get it. Can you explain it to me?"

I shake my head. "I'm sorry. Maybe another time—" I start walking again, trying to get away from him, but he just follows me.

"You know, I've read some of the stuff that you gave me, and it opened my eyes to a lot of things I didn't know about before."

"Aha," I nod and scan the cars around me. *Where is that damn car?* I have no idea where I left it.

"You know what I think?" He steps in front of me, blocking my way, so I have no choice but to stop.

"What?" I ask tersely.

He looks inside my cart and pauses, clearly confused. "Wow! Did you buy the whole supply of kale? Is that for your rabbits or something?"

"I like to make green smoothies," I reply. "You should try them sometime."

"Maybe I will," he nods.

I push the cart, but he doesn't let me through.

"You may be feeling so superior, but I think you're using animals, just like everyone else."

I puff angrily, the nerve this guy has to accuse me of such a thing.

I push harder, trying to pass him, but he keeps looking at me with these annoying blue eyes of his.

"You're using animals to hide from the real world and people," he says.

"Oh, and what's the real world? Where is it? Because it doesn't get much more real than what I see in the shelter."

He finally lets go of my cart, and I'm on the move again. He follows me and keeps talking, "What you do is admirable, but you're hiding from people. You're using animals as your shield. They've become the center of your attention. Doesn't your guru say that humans shouldn't depend on animals for relationships and to give our lives meaning?"

He did say that. (In one of the books I recommended to Ryan, professor Gary Francione says that people shouldn't have pets. And as much as I love my dogs, I have to admit that the whole pet breeding industry is simply another way of human oppression over animals.)

Wait a minute. Did he read the stuff I gave him?

"First of all, he is not my guru. Besides, I'm helping these animals. The animals need me just as much as I need them. They don't have a voice in this society."

"That's my point. To become their voice, you must be present and visible—in the human world. But just look at you. You quit your real job. You don't want any real relationships. You can't hide behind the animals all the time. Because if you do, then you're just using them for your own selfish purpose like the rest of us."

How dare he accuse me of being selfish! I gasp in indignation.

"And what's that selfish purpose exactly?" I ask.

"Personal satisfaction and fulfillment. Being above the rest of us. Feeling superior and the only one who's truly ethical and moral," he says. "Isn't that how you feel?"

I finally locate my vehicle and unlock the door.

"And you know what else I think?" he asks, helping me pack the groceries into my trunk.

I don't answer. I've had enough of his bright ideas.

"The truth is—you're just like the rest of us," he says with a smirk.

"I'm not the one who says one thing and does another," I say and slam the trunk shut.

"What are you talking about?" he asks as I get in, start the engine and drive away before he can see me crying.

I could have asked him about Anastasia; tell him I saw him with her the other day.

But I'm not going to beg for his attention.

It's not like we are married; we aren't even dating.

And that kiss meant nothing to him, I'm sure.

<h1 style="text-align:center">37.</h1>

I get on the highway and put on a record with my favorite rock band. I turn the up volume until it's almost deafening.

I keep pressing the gas pedal, trying to outrun my thoughts.

Why am I always falling for the wrong guy?

I thought we had so much in common. Ryan isn't vegan, but he risks his life for others every day. People and animals. And that's really something.

But now it's over. Before it even started.

He is a cheater, just like the rest of them.

And the shelter is going to close. The fundraiser is not going to be enough. It's all hopeless—what am I going to do with my life?

Suddenly, a truck cuts me off, and I veer to the left. I hold on to the steering wheel, trying not to panic.

The truck veers to the right and almost hits a van in the right lane. Is he drunk or something?

I hit the breaks with all the force I can muster, trying to avoid the collision, praying that the cars behind me manage to stop in time.

Everything is happening in slow motion, like in a movie, and I don't hear anything behind the music.

In the rearview mirror, I watch a van behind me getting closer.

Bam!

The van hits my car hard, pushing me off the road. I lose control and hit a traffic sign, and feel the world swirl around me.

Giving myself up to the higher power, I close my eyes. I hear another crash, and then everything stops.

I don't' feel any pain, but when I try to move, I can't. I open my eyes and see whiteness. Am I dead?

Do they play rock in heavens? Or wherever people go after death?

I am relieved, as I realize that it's just my airbag and that I'm fine.
Suddenly, I start laughing.
And screaming.
And crying.
The emotions pour out of me to the rhythm of the music.
I turn it off.
"Are you okay?" someone knocks on my window, concerned.
"I'm fine. Totally. Definitely," I reply.
"The ambulance will be here soon. The paramedics are going to examine you. They may take you to the hospital for a checkup."
And I'm like, what?
OMG. I must go home now.
Who's going to take care of the food?

38.

After the whole day spent waiting for the police and ambulances to arrive and then getting a checkup in the emergency room, all I wanted was to go to sleep. I practically collapsed in my bed and woke up at dawn, feeling a little soreness in my neck, but otherwise surprisingly well. My friend, Alexandra, agreed to deliver pierogi all the way from Brooklyn, so that problem was solved. And then in the morning, Patricia picked me up as my car was practically totaled.

The skies look gloomy but clear by the time we get to the site, and the sun is shining when the first guests start to arrive. I look around. The people from the Kind Heart shelter did all they could, but would that be enough? We're all nervous and anxious to see how many people will show up. Or are they going to end up at the other event, where the sponsors tempted them with their freebies?

Ugh! I'm so nervous and frustrated.

And so is Barbara Wiley, who keeps checking all the tables and displays. It's the day of the fundraiser, and everybody is nervous. It's a big deal. The morning is cloudy, and for a moment, it looks like rain, and there are even a few raindrops falling here and there. I walk the grounds and talk to the shelter employees, making sure they know what they are supposed to do. The volunteers are walking the dogs and trying to keep them busy. It's a new situation for them to be out of their kennels, where they usually spend their days.

Everything is ready. The tables have been set up with food, fliers, and merchandise for sale. The balloons and decorations are colorful and pretty. And all the volunteers and employees are here, wearing the brand new t-shirts, waiting at the ready.

There is only one problem.

It's already well past eleven, but hardly any visitors are here. I expected a lower than average turnout due to another event going on at the same time, but this? This is a disaster. There are more shelter employees and volunteers than visitors.

It looks like their worst fears were materializing. And where are the firefighters? Weren't they supposed to be there by now?

"Now, what?" Barbara says. "Can you try to find out what's going on?"

Is it because of the rumors? What if people believed them? Penelope made sure that local papers published our article about the shelter, where we addressed those insane accusations, but online people were still discussing it.

I can hear loud music blasting across the park; their DJ is going to wake the whole town. They seem to be having a fun party over there. In contrast, the atmosphere in our part of the park is dejected.

I overhear a few volunteers talking.

"Why aren't people coming?" one of them asks.

"Everybody is at that other event. Friends of Animals, or something," someone answers.

"We should have hired a DJ, too. Or at least have some music playing."

"I thought that Ryan Kowalski and his buddies would be here. We're never going to raise enough money if they don't show up."

"And look at all that food. Who's going to eat all that?"

The spirit among the crew is low. I try Ryan's phone number again and again, but it keeps going straight to his voice mail.

"I'll go and find out what's happening with the firefighters why they're not here yet," I say to Barbara.

"No. Stay here; I don't want you to disappear on me."

"I won't. I'll be back as soon as I find out what's going on."

But I already know.

The truck won't come. The firefighters won't come.

They're probably having so much fun at the other event; they forgot they were supposed to come here as well.

Men can't be trusted. Ryan can't be trusted. That's what happened. It's as simple as that.

I make up my mind to ask my father for the money. "The money may be dirty, but at least it will be for good use," I say to Eric.

"Maybe there'll be no need. Just look at that," Eric points his hand toward a commotion on the other side of the road.

A big crowd is marching toward us. And in the middle of it all is a big fire truck, decorated with balloons and banners, blasting loud music.

And then I see Ryan.

Yelling into a microphone, he asks everyone to join the local fire department in supporting the Kind Heart Animal Shelter.

And I just stand there with my mouth hanging open.

"They're here!" Barbara exhales a sigh of relief.

Penelope claps her hands, "Of course, they're here!"

Eric claps his hands, rolls his sleeves up, and shrieks, "Let's get rolling!"

39.

As it turned out, the other event didn't draw people away from our fundraiser. If anything, it helped to attract more visitors, because most people ended up attending both parties. The television and local papers all contributed to spreading the word. Even the unfortunate Morning Show didn't do much damage.

"Save the Kind Heart Shelter. Save our cats and dogs. Adopt, don't shop." The slogans are everywhere.

Most people came not just for the animals, but because they wanted to meet the firefighters. The line to purchase a mug, a t-shirt with signatures of the heroes, plus, of course, the calendar was several hundred yards long, and after just a few hours, everything sold out.

Even the food was spot on. With satisfaction, I noted that my food was disappearing faster than the rest of the dishes. It made me proud. After several disasters in that department, I made sure my food is not only delicious but also attractive. The presentation is key when it comes to events like that.

Pierogi and other food I ordered from the White Eagle were a hit. Plus, Eric prepared delicious barbecued cauliflower bits in hot sauce, vegetables marinated and grilled to perfection, mushrooms, and fruits, pineapple, tomatoes, zucchini. He also brought hummus, bread, and vegan cupcakes. And his smoked tofu spread—was smoking!

The success exceeded our expectations.

People often complain that plain tofu is boring. But the thing about tofu is you either love it or you haven't prepared it well. Of course, no one would eat meat without spices or soup without salt and pepper, but somehow everybody expects plant foods to be precisely right from the get-go—so how is that even fair? Nobody thinks about the fact that meat or eggs or any other ingredient without any spices are bland.

Except for fruit, of course. Deliciously ripe mango, for example, is heavenly right out of the skin and doesn't need any improvements, in my opinion. I love ripe fruits for dessert more than anything else—strawberries, cherries, raspberries, blueberries, peaches, and mango, which is my favorite.

And best of all, many families declared the will to adopt and help out. A few of the dogs have been adopted on the spot. Of course, the families still have to go through the vetting process, but they fell in love with the dogs we brought to the event.

We're ecstatic. The future suddenly doesn't seem so gloomy. I'm tired but, for the first time in a long time, truly happy.

"Good thing, we set up an online store and online donation buttons. You did a great job, Penelope," Barbara says.

"We didn't anticipate the demand, but a lot of the orders were made online," Penelope says.

"So how much did we make?" I ask.

"We did great."

"But how much? Will it be enough?"

"Almost fifty thousand dollars!"

"Wow! That's fantastic!" I exclaim and clap my hands.

"Yes, and I want to thank you all," Barbara says. "It was a tremendous success. People showed in big numbers. Best of all, we have dozens of applications for dog adoptions."

"Who is Ryan talking to over there? Zara asks.

"Is that Anastasia, the Zumba girl?"

"Yes, it is," I say. There we go again, I think wryly. I turn around and start cleaning the trash. I'm done with men, the voice inside my head reminds me.

40.

Penelope shrugs, "It's probably nothing."

I sigh. "Yeah, it's nothing. As in nothing is between us." I growl.

I should have known. Why was I even getting my hopes up?

"Didn't he tell you he wasn't seeing anyone?" Zara asks.

I shrug. "As if that ever meant anything when a guy said so."

Zara shakes her head. "He doesn't seem like the type to me. One who'd need to lie to get a girl."

"It's in their nature. They just can't NOT lie," I declare.

I notice Barbara's face changes expression as she's talking to someone on the phone. She finishes the call and shrieks, "Oh my god!"

We all look at her, alarmed.

"What's wrong, Barbara?" Eric asks.

"I just talked to the owner of the property we're renting. He said he changed his mind. He isn't selling!"

I gasp. "What? I don't believe it. How did that happen?"

"It turns out your father knows our landlord and convinced him not to sell!"

I shake my head. "But how?"

"I have no idea. And I don't care. That's such great news!"

She's right. With the fundraiser being a success, and the owner deciding not to sell, things are finally up for the shelter.

I look in the direction of Ryan. He's surrounded by people, mostly women, talking and signing the calendars and t-shirts, like a celebrity.

He notices me and waves his hand, and I want to run away and hide somewhere where no one would find me, but he's already heading toward me, with his big smile, pulling the Zumba girl behind him.

"Olivia, I'd like you to meet my sister, Anastasia. Anastasia, this is Olivia."

"I believe we've met," Anastasia says, without a hint of irony or sarcasm.

"Your sister?" I ask, shocked. "But, I thought …"

"Step-sister, actually," Anastasia explains.

"She works for the pet shop. And she's doing yoga classes for the rescue workers."

Anastasia is his niece?

"I have a surprise for you," Ryan says, showing me his phone.

"What's that?" I ask, not understanding.

I see a picture of Ruffy on the screen and gasp. "Did you find him?"

Ryan nods.

"That's wonderful! Where is he now? Can I see him?"

"He's at my place. Do I deserve a kiss now?"

"Of course, you do!" I gush and give him the most passionate kiss in my life. The world around me starts swirling.

Whoa! Did I just die and went to heaven?

I walk back to our table, and he follows me. "Let me take you home," he says as we step outside into the parking lot. "Do you want to see Ruffy? He's doing great."

"Sure, I'd love to see how Ruffy is doing," I say. Then I look around. I can't leave now. "How about tomorrow?" I ask.

"Tomorrow it is," Ryan nods. "We'll be waiting."

41.

When I get back home, I'm exhausted. I turn on the television and watch the coverage of our event. Barbara is being interviewed, thanking all the people who participated for their generous donations. "The Kind Heart Animal Shelter has just celebrated a fantastic milestone: As of this afternoon, all of our kennels are empty. We adopted most of the dogs and cats in our care."

"So, what happens when your last available dog gets adopted?" the reporter asks her.

"Your staff and volunteers jump into the kennels to celebrate! Seeing so many pets find wonderful new homes is what makes it all worthwhile for us. We've adopted out 25 cats and 33 dogs so far as a result of the event. Plus, the shelter has been running a promotion where adoption fees for cats and dogs aged five and above are waived. We still have dogs and cats waiting for good homes, so keep those adoptions coming!" Barbara says and continues, "We can't thank our donors enough for making this promotion possible. And we would also like to thank the whole community for adopting and helping us get so many deserving cats and dogs into new homes for the holidays."

I look at the envelope lying on my desk with my father's check. Since the shelter is doing better, perhaps I should use the money to find my own place and pay off my student loan?

My phone plays a happy jingle. I look at the screen; it's Sebastian.

"We need your help," he says. "Our office is understaffed. We represent several the animal rights activists suing the abusive breeder," Sebastian says. "I think you'll be a great fit. Will you join our team?"

"I will," I reply.

And just like that, I decide to go back to law.

I decide to make myself some juice to toast to that. But what to do with that pulp? I sit at my laptop and search for ways to use the vegetable pulp left after juicing. A whole page of suggestions pops up—recipes for sauces, cakes, veggie burgers, pies, and pates.

One recipe catches my attention, so I click on it and decide to try it. Even though I won't be able to use the whole pulp, it sounds promising and might be worth trying.

42.

From the way Ruffy greets me at the door, I can tell that he is okay. And he absolutely adores Ryan!

I'm amazed it happened so quickly; I didn't think he would trust him so easily. This adopted pit bull can't stop hugging his new caretaker. Women at the shelter may have cooed over this picture, but the real-life image is so much more enticing and sexy.

What's going on with you, Olivia? I scold myself. Why do you have all these feelings for that man?

"He's such a love bug, honestly," Ryan says. "I'll be lying there, and he'll put his head under my arm, or his paw over my chest. And he'll even lay on my chest."

They look adorable together. I snap a picture of them lying on the sofa. I have to admit they're a perfect match.

"He missed you," Ryan says. He wraps his arms around both of us and gently kisses me on my lips.

What is he doing? I don't need another failed relationship. I'm done with men; I keep reminding myself. To no avail.

I can't move, as I don't want to startle the dog sleeping on my lap.

Ryan notices my hesitation. "Don't worry; I'm not going to hurt you."

THE END

Recipes

Lentil and Vegetable Pate with Cranberries

Prep time: 20 minutes + 45 minutes baking

Ingredients:
2 onions
2 bay leaves
2 grains of allspice
2 cloves
Oil

1 cup cooked brown or green lentils
1 cup vegetable pulp (carrots, beets, celery roots, apples, etc.)
1 cup of cooked millet
½ cup of oil
2 - 3 tablespoons of soy sauce
¾ teaspoon of marjoram
½ teaspoon of savory
1/4 teaspoon of lovage
a pinch of nutmeg
salt and black pepper

4 tablespoons of dried cranberries
a baking pan approximately 8 x 4 inches

Method:
Preheat the oven to 360 degrees (180 degrees Celsius).
Dice the onion, heat the oil in a frying pan, and add the onion together with the bay leaf, allspice, and cloves. Cook over low heat for 4-6 minutes until the onion is soft and translucent; then remove the spices and discard.

In a large mixing bowl, combine the cooked lentils with the vegetable pulp, onions, millet, oil, soy sauce, a pinch of salt, and the rest of the spices. Mix with a hand blender until smooth; taste and season with more salt if needed. Add cranberries and mix them into the mass.

Spoon the mass into the pan lined with baking paper, even out, and bake for 35-45 minutes. The pate will be very soft inside after baking. Let it cool for a few hours or overnight. Serve with bread or toast.

Tips:
For the pate not to have a moist bottom, bake it in a mold greased with oil and coarsely sprinkled with breadcrumbs or in the gluten-free version with ground nuts.

If the pate does not have a golden top after the time has elapsed, bake it for another 10-15 minutes.

(Recipe inspired by Jadlonomia.com)

Green Berry Banana Smoothie

2 cups of water

2 very ripe bananas

1 cup of strawberries or blueberries or raspberries (fresh or frozen)

2 celery stalks

4 leaves kale or 2 cups of tightly packed greens

Put in your blender container and blend on the highest setting until smooth. (Kale may be a little tough for some blenders, so you may use softer greens, such as spinach or baby green mix.)

Fresh Vegetable Juice

4 carrots

2 celery stalks

½ beet

1 apple

Pass through your juicer and enjoy!

Thank you!

Thank you for reading!

If you enjoyed the story, please remember to leave a positive rating and review it on <u>Amazon's page</u>. A glowing review will make my day!

A Taste of Love: Eat, Love, Vegan

It was supposed to be a MAKEOVER of her family RESTAURANT, not her LIFE.

A clean romantic comedy with a touch of romance plus some delicious vegan recipes.

When Alexandra agrees to take care of the family restaurant, she thinks it's only temporary until her father recovers from a massive heart attack.

What she doesn't know is that the restaurant is in trouble, and participating in the Xtreme Restaurant Makeover television show may be the only way to save it.

The show is hosted by a hot but cutthroat celebrity chef, Russell Stone, who turns around failing restaurants in less than five days, but his style and manners (or lack of thereof) are hard for Alexandra to swallow.

Dirty pots and pans are flying around the kitchen, food gets spit out, and interiors are gutted as millions are watching and cheering. The bigger the restaurant owner's humiliation, the higher the ratings.

She despises the very idea of it and doesn't think she could do it. Or could she?

A Taste of Love: Eat, Love, Vegan is available <u>on Amazon</u>.

About the Author

Joanna Slodownik is the author of fiction and non-fiction books that keep kids and adults around the world entertained, informed, and inspired. Joanna Slodownik was born in Warsaw, Poland, but lived for most of her life in New Jersey. Now she's back to Warsaw, where she lives with her son, Adam, her husband, and Ramses, the dog adopted from the shelter. When she's not writing and plotting her books and stories, she's taking walks with Ramses, biking around town, making green smoothies, and cooking vegan meals for her family. Check out her blogs greenreset.com and joannaslodownik.com.

Your Gifts Are Waiting!

Get a free excerpt of the "Hearts on Fire (Dogs, Love, and Heroes; Calendar Men)," the "7-Day Green Reset Challenge" ebook (with my recipes, shopping lists, tips, detox advice, and more), plus be notified about hot new releases. Go to JoannaSlodownik.com/gift/